Scratch

SKYE MACKINNON

CONTENTS

BLURB

Men are just like cats. They don't do what they're told and constantly want cuddles.

Kat misses her solitary assassin life. Instead of doing one cold-hearted kill after another, she now has to deal with two and a half men all vying for her attention. But with a new crisis emerging, she doesn't have time for one relationship, let alone three.
Kittens are being taken, including Ryker's son. Is there a killer on the loose or is someone trying to get Kat's attention?

The second book in this purrfectly exciting urban fantasy series.

AUTHOR'S NOTE

No animals were harmed in the making of this book. On the contrary, two bunnies got a lot of cuddles (and in return, they nibbled holes into the author's socks).

However, there are some scenes that animal lovers might find upsetting.

As you will know from the first book in the series, this book is set in a world very similar to our own, but there are some deciding differences. Technology has developed differently, and while there are many devices you may be used to, such as televisions, there are no mobile phones, cars or the internet. No guns, either.

This book is written in British English and uses some British expressions and idioms. Please don't see these as spelling mistakes. We say mum rather than mom, use a lot of 's' instead of 'z' (cosy, realise, …) and use 'got' as the past participle of 'get' (instead of 'gotten').

And finally, subscribe to Skye's newsletter for updates about new releases: skyemackinnon.com/newsletter

*In memory of Mitza, also known as Muffin, Cucumber and other
food related names.
Your purring is greatly missed.*

CHAPTER ONE

It's official. I've turned into a crazy cat lady. The horde of kittens at my feet is living proof of that.

Seven kittens of all colours and shapes. I was told that they were all from the same litter, but even though I know it's possible, I'm having a hard time believing that. One ginger kitten has a coat so fluffy that his eyes were hardly visible underneath all that fur. A sibling – if it is indeed related – has barely any hair at all, looking very naked. I think it's supposed to be like that, but that doesn't stop me from thinking that someone should knit a blanket for it.

Not me, obviously. The only thing I use knitting needles for is to poke out eyes. They're quite efficient at that.

"What am I going to do with you?" I mutter, staring down at the kittens. They were delivered to me anonymously, with nothing but a bag of cat food and a handwritten note. A 'donation', they called it. I shake my head in disbelief. A donation of seven kittens. Not exactly what I need just now. I've got enough to deal with without a bunch of furry fluff balls meowing for attention.

"Cats!"

Benjamin runs down the stairs, excitement written all over his face. Alright, if I'm the crazy cat lady, he's reached an entirely different level of craziness. The deluded cat gentleman?

I now leave all of the feeding and petting duties to him, although I do offer occasional cuddles. Not many of the cats accept that from me. They're proud animals, and because I understand their language, I'm not quite the same as a human petting them. With Benjamin, they can pretend to be nothing but fluffy animals but, with me, they have to prove how intelligent and kick-arse they are. Luckily, these kittens haven't learned that distinction yet, and they rub against my legs, vying for cuddles.

"They were delivered an hour ago," I tell Benjamin. "Don't suppose you know anything about that?"

Other people wouldn't notice the slight twitch of his right eyelid, but I'm a professional.

"Benjamin?!"

He shrugs. "I told a friend that I was looking after some stray cats. Maybe it was him."

I glare at him. "You told a friend where we live?"

"Don't look at me like that. He knows already. He's referred a few of our clients, actually."

One of the kittens is trying to climb up my leg and I gently pick it up, cradling it in my arms.

"Kittens, eh?" I sigh. "They're your responsibility. If

you can't deal with them, I'll tell one of the adult cats and they'll add them to their family."

Benjamin grins happily. "They'll want for nothing."

"As long as Meow doesn't want for nothing either," I warn him. "Remember, this is still a business, no matter how many cats live in this house. We are *not* an animal shelter."

I leave him to it, taking the kitten with me. She's a glossy black with bright blue eyes lined with silver. Unusual and absolutely striking.

"Do you have a name yet?" I ask, but she's too young to understand. She can't be older than a couple of weeks, and cats don't develop the ability to understand me in human form until they're around eight weeks old. I could shift, but I might have to do that soon and doing it twice will take too much energy.

I dread that shift. Not because of the shifting, but because of the conversation I'm going to have. With Ryker. The cat who isn't a cat. Who's deceived me ever since we met. Granted, he never actually looked at me and lied to my face by saying, "I'm Ryker, I'm a cat, I'm not a shifter," but it should be simple feline decency to tell a fellow shifter one's species.

He's been out of town for a couple of days, long enough for me to practice our conversation again and again. Still, I'm not feeling prepared at all. I've distracted myself by cleaning up the last of the Healers mess. We've destroyed their labs and research, checked in with the children who got poisoned and were given the antidote, and killed quite a few people. Lennox, Gryphon and I have become quite a good team. Luckily, we've been so busy that I haven't had the time to think about feelings. Emotions. Attractions.

I'm going to avoid dealing with that for as long as I possibly can. Life is difficult enough without getting attached to people.

Now that all traces of the Healers have been eradicated, life will hopefully return to normal. I've got several contracts lined up. Good old assassinations, nothing special. I'm glad. I won't do any more investigations any time soon. Not after this experience. Of course, I'm happy that we got to help all those children, but I don't want to get involved in things like that again. Ever since starting Meow, I've been trying to keep a low profile, keep out of sight from the Pack, but I'm afraid that this case may have thrown waves that I can't take back.

Lennox is pestering me about making plans to attack the Pack for selling children for experiments, but I'm wary. We're not strong enough to face them, even with Gryphon on our side. Three against a hundred or more isn't feasible really.

I retreat to my office, the kitten purring in my arms. I sit her on my lap and take a look at my mail. The boring part of running a business. Bills, bills and more bills. Mr Kindler's brother still hasn't paid me. I made quite a bit of money during the investigation because the baddies kept leaving their cash lying around, but I rely on clients paying their fees. I'll send him one more reminder and if he doesn't give me what he owes, I'll pay him a visit with my knives. I doubt he was involved in the poisonings, otherwise, he wouldn't have wanted anyone to look into his brother's death, but I won't have any pity for him if he doesn't pay.

There's one letter with a familiar symbol pressed into the thick paper. A snake biting its own tail. My mysterious benefactor. I've not heard from him since he told me that his granddaughter died. To be honest, I'm quite glad about that. I wouldn't know what to say to him. 'My condolences' doesn't quite cut it.

I open the envelope with one of my knives – this one was in a sheath wrapped around my lower thigh – and take out the letter. Ink stains are blotted all around the edges. I didn't think Mystery Man was the kind of person to send such an untidy letter. His clothes were always immaculate, all the way from his top hat down to his perfectly polished shoes.

To whom it may concern.

My father died two days ago. While going through his accounts I found that he'd given you full usage of one of his properties. Since I don't want to get involved in that side of his business, I shall give you the deeds of this house in return of a full non-disclosure agreement as well as an assurance of no future demands for money or assistance.

Please find corresponding documents attached.

I read it again. And again.

The house is mine. Even though Mystery Man had made it sound like it was mine to keep when we first met, I always had it at the back of my mind that one day, he might want it back. Now, that worry can disappear.

Oh. And he's dead. Such a pity. Should I send

flowers? Is that what you do when you didn't kill the person who's died?

I should probably feel sad, but I don't. I didn't really know him. He always stayed a mystery. I'm grateful to him, very, but that's not really enough to make me sad. Especially when the house is now officially mine.

I take a quick look at the contract and papers the daughter sent and sign them straight away. I don't think I'm going to get a better offer. I put the letter on my out-tray – yes, I actually have one, I can't believe it myself – and decide that it's enough office work for one day. I need to do some finances at some point, but not today. I'm in mourning. That's my excuse.

The little kitten meows.

"Yes, I've not forgotten you," I mutter and tickle her head. She immediately starts purring again. Such a cutie.

I hear Lily long before she enters the office. Without knocking, obviously.

"You two are very cute," she says with a look at the kitten in my lap. "Want some catnip?"

The kitten stares at her unimpressed, then continues licking my arm. She doesn't know the pleasures of catnip yet. I shall have to introduce her. Although, no. I'd have to share. I'm not the sharing kind, especially when it comes to catnip. That stuff is the food of the Purry Gods. Lily is the only one who knows of my slight addiction.

"Catnip?" I ask, pretending to be all cool about it. "Where?"

She laughs evilly. "I was kidding. You'll have to get

your own. I'm not aiding your drug habit, not after last time."

I'm almost embarrassed about that incident. Almost. In the end, nobody should care about me rolling on the floor with a ball of yarn. While being human. Happens all the time, right?

Lily leans against the wall, one of her muddy boots leaving traces on the wallpaper. Before, I wouldn't have cared but now this is my house. My property.

"Feet off the walls," I growl and she raises an eyebrow.

"What's going on?"

I shrug. "Mystery man died, this house is mine now. No mud on the walls. No mud on the floor. No blood anywhere besides the basement. Got it?"

She grins. "You own a house? Like an actual person? Like someone who has a job and goes to work and watches tv and doesn't kill people?"

"Seems like it. I just hope that doesn't mean that I have to pay tax and get an insurance and all that crap."

Lily laughs. "I can't imagine you comparing insurance prices. Ben might enjoy doing that though. I hadn't realised how much he enjoys numbers until he went through all those Kindler documents."

"All his. I wonder if there's an insurance against attacks by hordes of enslaved shifters. That might come in handy."

Her smile disappears. "Do you think the Pack is going to attack us?"

"It's always been just a matter of time," I reply with a sigh. "I think they knew that I had the support of someone powerful, so they waited until they had more information. Once they find out that Mystery Man has died and that nobody is protecting me, they'll come to get me back. They can't let me make a precedent by escaping their rule. If that news spread, they'd have a rebellion to deal with."

"Maybe we should be the ones to start it," Lily says thoughtfully.

"Huh?"

"The rebellion. If you go out in the open, let the Pack members know that it's possible to remove their collars and have a life of freedom, you might distract their leaders enough not to come for you."

I groan. "You sound like Lennox. He wants me to take the fight to the Pack as well."

Lily grins and pushes herself off the wall. "Good. Now I just need to get the others on my side and then we'll make you see reason."

I don't tell her that I'm tempted by the idea of going against the Pack. There are reasons why I shouldn't even consider it, reasons the others don't know about.

"By the way," Lily begins and walks over to my desk, leaning forward until I can see her boobs and her devilish smile.

"What do you want?"

She flutters her eyelashes at me. Seriously? She should know by now that this isn't the way to sway me. As attractive as she is, she's not my type.

"So... I know we don't have an employment contract..."

"Do you want a raise?" I ask suspiciously, but she shakes her head.

"A holiday."

I think my eyes are about to pop out of their sockets. A holiday? Is there anything more mundane?

"Why?" I ask weakly. I've never had a holiday in all my life and I was assuming that it was the same for Lily. Even the idea of taking a few days off... actually, it's very tempting. I'm a business owner though. Self-employed. There are no days off. Death needs to happen regularly.

"There's a thing I want to go to," she says, evading my eyes. "It's a... well, it's something I've always wanted to do."

"Details," I demand, more out of curiosity than being a strict boss. Of course, she can have a holiday. I don't really care. Well, I care that she isn't inviting me, but that's another matter.

"It's a convention," she mutters. "For people like me."

"Poison-loving assassins?"

"Do I really need to spell it out for you?" She sighs. "It's a succubi meetup."

I gape at her. "Succubi? But you always said they don't exist. Whenever I suggested that you might be an incubus, you... you lied to me!"

She shakes her head, still evading my eyes. "Incubus. You've always called me an incubus and they don't exist. They'd be the male equivalents of a succubus, but they aren't real. Succubi on the other hand... Well, I'm sorry. I'm so used not to telling people and so, of course, I didn't want to tell you when we first met. And then by the time we became friends, it felt too late."

She finally looks at me, exposing her vulnerability. If I were someone else, I'd give her a hug.

Instead, I just stare at her while gathering my thoughts. She's lied to me, but then, so have I. Just like her, I'm used to not telling the truth, bending it, omitting important details. I shouldn't feel as hurt as I do.

"I'm sorry," she repeats. "I should have told you."

I sigh. "It's not like I didn't suspect. I just thought you didn't know or didn't want to admit it to yourself."

Lily shakes her head. "I was born into a succubus family and I went to one of their schools. I was trained to seduce, but I've always been more interested in poisons and assassinations. I dropped out of the academy and turned away from the succubus life, trying to become something else, someone I wanted to be, not who my upbringing dictated. But I miss my family and thought it might be a good idea to go to the annual succubus convention."

I give her a small smile. It does sound like something she should do. It sounds way too social for me, but Lily is different. She loves being surrounded by other people, while I have always preferred my own company.

"If I'm to give you a few days off, you have to answer my questions," I say, my smile turning into a grin. "And trust me, I want to learn all there is to know about succubi."

CHAPTER TWO

We end up in the living room with four packs of crisp and one half-empty bag of toffee popcorn.

"So there are no male succubi?" I ask for the second time. It still boggles my mind.

"Nope, succubi only have female offspring," Lily repeats. "We use human men to get us pregnant, but then they're no longer needed and it's all down to the women. Usually, several generations of succubi live together and help look after each others' daughters."

"Does that mean you don't know your father?"

"No idea who he is. He was a sperm donor, basically. I don't really care about who he was, although I'm rather grateful for his good genes. My mum is tiny so I must get my tallness from him."

"And there's actually an academy for succubi?" I ask with a laugh. "Is it basically one big sex thing?"

She shakes her head. "Sex is the smallest part of it all. We don't actually need to sleep with the people we feed off. Seduction can be much more efficient. Imagine it as the main course. Play with their feelings, get their hopes up, flirt a little, increase the tension, then fuck them for dessert."

"Sounds fun."

She grins, reminding me of the predator that she is. "Totally. I may have dropped out of the academy, but I'm an expert at seduction nonetheless. Sadly, it only works on humans, otherwise, I would have been able to take my holiday without divulging all my secrets."

She winks at me. "Can I go? It's only going to be a couple of days. Unless I find some boy toys to play with, obviously. I'm thinking some rich guys to get some money from to repaint my bedroom."

"Again?" I groan. "You've redecorated that at least four times in as many months."

Lily shrugs. "I like to change things up a little. Having the same colour walls gets boring."

Right now, her room is entirely black with some dark red drapings in the corners. Not really my style. I'd go for all black.

The sound of the front door opening interrupts our conversation. I sniff the air. Gryphon. His scent is easy to recognise. Full of testosterone and suppressed anger. He's a bowstring waiting to snap. I'm going to have to make sure I'm not in the way when it happens. He seems all funny and jovial when he talks to me, but my cat senses keep warning me about the tension in him. There's something he's hiding, and I need to find out what it is.

I don't like secrets, at least not when it's other people

having them. I'm full of secrets, but that's a good thing. It's boring to tell other people everything about your life. Where's the fun in that? Besides, there are some things I'm not proud of, and that says a lot.

"Who is it?" Lily asks, reminding me that she doesn't have the same shifter senses that I have. I'll have to ask her about her succubus skills later on. Is it just seduction or is there more to it?

"Me."

Gryphon enters the room before I can answer. He's all in black as usual, but rather than having his dark hair in a ponytail or in a bun, it falls onto his shoulders and ends around his collarbones. That answers the question I've had ever since I met him. Yes, his hair is longer than mine. Impressive. It's silkier than mine too. Mine would probably be shinier if I washed it more often, but my looks aren't very important to me. The dead don't care if their killer wore makeup or had frizzy hair.

"I shall leave you to it."

Lily slips out of the door before I can ask her to stay. Damn. I'd hoped not to be alone with Gryphon. He makes me feel uneasy. Not in a bad way, necessarily, but I don't know how to act around him. Yes, he makes me insecure. I admit it. Question is how to deal with that. Avoiding being alone with him has worked until now, but with Lily gone, I'll have to woman up and face him.

He sits down on the sofa opposite me, then gets up again, removing an empty crisp bag from below his bum. I never claimed that anyone in this house is tidy or cleans up after themselves.

"Why are you here?" I ask, a little surprised at how

hostile I sound. I need to tone it down. I don't want him to realise how uncomfortable he makes me feel.

"I was in the neighbourhood and thought I'd pop in," he says with a disarming grin. "How are things?"

"I can smell your lie," I retort, giving him a stern stare. "Why did you really come?"

His grin widens. "I was bored."

I sigh. "Lie, again. Tell me the truth or I'll throw you out. I'm busy enough as it is."

"You're not a very gracious host, you know that, right?"

"I'm not a polite person," I snap back. "Now get out before I practice my knife throwing skills on you."

He snickers. "Touchy. I guess it might make you happy to hear that I need your help."

I raise an eyebrow. "You? My help?"

Gryphon laughs. "Yes, me. Trust me, this wasn't my idea, but since you're the only assassin who comes close my own level of perfection-"

"Close?!" I interrupt him. "I'm miles better than you."

I catch the dart he throws at me just before it pricks my shoulder. Lucky for me, he's not as quick and my dart nips his chin. A drop of blood falls onto his black shirt. Bingo.

Then I realise that we both threw darts at the same time. Like we think in a similar way. Nope. Not going down that route. I've worked hard to be different from others, even other assassins. It's the only way to stay unpredictable. Let's hope this was just a coincidence and not the start of a pattern.

"Poisoned?" he asks and sniffs at the dart.

"No, you'll be fine." I lean back and cross my arms behind my head. "What do you need my help with?"

Now that I bested him, I feel a lot more confident. He wants my help, which gives me the upper hand. Maybe I'll have him grovel on the floor, kissing my feet. After that, he wouldn't think that he's better than me.

"It's a girl," he begins and I stare at him in disbelief.

"You want dating advice from me?"

He laughs. "No, not that kind of girl. She's definitely not my type. She's too... innocent. She's a neighbour and someone's stolen her necklace."

I shake my head. "I don't do investigating. That was a one-off, from now on it's back to killing. No more cases to solve, no more riddles, no more headaches."

"If you find who the thief is, you get to kill them," he offers.

I laugh. "I was told the same thing last time too. If I'd listened, you'd be dead now."

He looks a little disappointed. "I'm sure I could find some cash if you need a reward."

"I've got enough darems for now, thanks. I'm really not interested. I just want things to go back to how they were."

"Mindless killing?" He smiles knowingly, although the disappointment is still evident in his voice.

"Exactly. Someone tells me who to kill, I do it, I get paid. Easy. No running around searching for clues, no interrogating, no conspiracies. Just look at the chaos this investigation has left us with. Even now, there are still ends to tie up. No, I don't want this again. Sorry." I smile at him to soften my words a little. I've seen other people do that so it's worth a try. Not sure why curving your lips has such an effect on people, but oh well, I'm used to not understanding why they behave the way they do. In a perfect world, everyone would just say what they mean and not rely on meaningless gestures and smiles. "I'm sure you can find someone else to look into it."

He stares at me intently, as if he's deciding whether this is my final word or not. I meet his eyes confidently. I'm not going to back down. I've already given Lily a favour by letting her take a holiday. Now it's time to be selfish. I've been behaving too human recently. I need to find my inner cat again.

Gryphon nods curtly and gets up. "You know where to find me if you change your mind."

He leaves me with a strange feeling. Guilt? Nah, that can't be. There's nothing I should have to feel guilty for. And no, I'm not feeling lonely either. I don't want him to stay and talk and become friends. Not in the slightest.

Luckily, a meow distracts me from my thoughts. It's Nyx, her beautiful white fur all silky and shiny. If she was a human, I bet everyone would ask her what kind of product she uses on her hair. Since she's a cat... guess her saliva is particularly good.

"What's up?" I ask her as she rubs against my legs, purring in contentment. "Have you been fed?"

She purrs her affirmation. I'm surprised. In her place, I would have said no to get more food. An honest cat, who would have thought.

Nyx meows and jumps onto the sofa, looking at me expectantly.

"Ryker?" I ask and she nods. Damn it. I'd hoped I would have more time. I sigh and get up. Of course, Nyx immediately takes my place, stretching out on the warm sofa. Cats. They know how to indulge.

❀ ❀ ❀ ❀ ❀ ❀

Ryker is waiting for me in the backyard. None of the other cats are here, it's just the two of us.

He's even more impressive than I remember him. His fur around his neck is so bushy that it resembles a lion's mane. His yellow eyes stare at me with an intensity that makes a shiver run down my back. It's time to face the music.

I sigh and shift, my body stretching in ways entirely unnatural. When whiskers pop out of my cheeks, I swipe at them with my oversized paws. It tickles, although I kind of love having whiskers. They add an entirely new sense to the mix.

"I've been told you want to talk to me," Ryker says in his deep, melodious voice. "What's this about?"

Is he pretending not to know? I thought that he was avoiding me the past few days, but now that he's there, I see no avoidance in those golden eyes of his. On the contrary, he's staring at me with both respect and curiosity.

"You lied to me," I start, then realise that actually, he didn't. "Or at least you omitted the truth."

His ears flick in confusion. "What are you talking

17

about? I keep a lot of secrets as part of looking after my family, but none of them concern you enough to make you this upset."

Upset? Well, maybe I am. Shifters should identify themselves to each other. It's easy to spot shifters walking around in their human form, but as animals, they're much harder to find. Right now, so shortly after shifting, other shifters would know because I still smell of human, but after a couple of hours, that scent will have mostly disappeared.

"What's wrong?" Ryker asks again. I don't know how to respond. For once in my life, I'm lost for words. I don't want to lose his support and loyalty, but I also can't stay quiet and just let him get away with it.

"You didn't tell me what you are," I finally say. "It would have been nice to know."

He blinks at me. "What I am? Isn't it obvious?"

"It wasn't to me. You should have told me." I suppress a growl.

He shakes his head. "I still don't know what you're talking about. I'm a cat. I thought every idiot could see that. Look, I have a tail." He flicks it in an almost alluring manner. I curse my mind for interpreting his movement in that way.

This time, I growl, the sound echoing in the enclosed space. "You're not *just* a cat though, are you."

Instead of explaining himself, he starts to laugh. It's a beautiful and very rare sound. Cats seldom laugh. Their lives are too sombre for that.

"I'm a cat. Nothing but a cat. I was born a cat and I

will die a cat. Now please, explain what the noisy kittens you're on about."

Noisy kittens? Of course, Ryker would be too posh to swear. He's that kind of cat.

Guess there's no way around it. "You're a shifter," I throw at him accusingly. "You're like me and you never said."

His laugh stops and he stares at me, blinking several times. "Where on earth did you get that idea?"

"Your blood. Lily tested it and it shows that you've got the shifter gene. You're the same as me. Now stop denying it and shift! I want to have a proper conversation with you, not this charade you've been keeping up."

Ryker takes a step back. His fur gets even more bushy as he takes on a pounce-ready stance.

"I'm not," he stutters, his confidence all but gone. "I'm a cat." He looks down at his paws and extends his claws. "See? I'm a cat. I've always been a cat. I'm not like you. I'm a cat. I'm a cat."

He continues to repeat it and that's what convinces me that he really didn't know. I'm good enough at reading both cats and humans to see his confusion for what it is.

"You're wrong," he mutters. "It can't be. I'd know."

I don't know what to do. Of all the different scenarios I'd imagined, this wasn't one of them. I'd thought he might deny it, but because he didn't want me to know, not because he didn't have a clue himself.

"Blood doesn't lie," I say gently. "You're a shifter.

How can you not know? Your parents must have been shifters, they must have told you?"

He looks at me, his eyes suddenly filled with sadness. "I'm a stray. I grew up on the streets, I never knew my parents. I've never had anything to do with humans or shifters until I met you. I'm a cat, I'm telling you. Take more of my blood. Test it again."

The urge to get closer, to rub my body against his in a gesture of comfort, is getting strong but I resist it. He needs to get through this on his own. I won't be of any help to him. Well, I can already see that I'll need to help him a lot to become a proper shifter, but right in this moment, he needs to deal with reality on his own.

"We can do that," I reply calmly, "but I doubt it will change anything. I've always thought you were too aware, too intelligent for a cat. Too empathetic. Normal cats wouldn't start a family and look after abandoned kittens. You doing that is proof that you're not just a cat. You've got a human side to you that we need to explore."

"We?" he asks sharply, but then sighs. "I guess you're right. There have been times when I felt out of place, like I was different from the other cats. I ignored it most of the time, but now that I think of it…"

Without warning, he jumps up the wall. He turns and looks down at me with his intense yellow eyes.

"I need some time to mull it over. I'll be back."

With that, he's gone, leaving me more confused than ever.

How the fuck am I going to turn a cat into a shifter?

CHAPTER THREE

Life is complicated. Some days, I wish I was nothing but a cat. A panther. Whatever. Sunbathing, eating, relaxing, snoozing the day away. Hunting butterflies, rubbing against a random stranger's legs, then some more sleeping.

Instead, I'm pacing back and forth, trying to sort out my thoughts. I'm alone in the house and I'm glad about it. I don't want any of the others to see me in this state of confusion. I'm always composed, always got a cool exterior, but now... I'm not sure if I want to throw something, kill someone or eat mountains of ice cream. Probably all three at the same time. Throw ice cream at someone to kill them, then eat it.

I'm going crazy. Thinking of using ice cream as a murder weapon. How terribly inefficient. Not even a complete beginner would come up with such a rubbish idea. Something's really wrong with me. I need to get back into the zone, get rid of all the confusing thoughts and feelings.

I run into my office and take a random file from my stack. I need to kill.

It's a simple assassination, a businessman who's got involved with the wrong people. They pay well and it sounds easy enough. They'd prefer poison but anything goes as long as it doesn't leave a giant mess. No problem. I open the hidden cabinet behind a horrendous painting of a highland cow (it came with the house) and take some knives and darts. I always have a few poison darts sewn into my clothes anyway, but it's always good to have more than I need. You never know who you might meet out there.

Equipped with more knives than most people have in their kitchen drawers, I leave the house, immediately taking to the roofs. It's late afternoon and not the perfect day for a hit, but I don't want to wait any longer. I need the rush of adrenaline, the feeling of complete control as I make my body jump from roof to roof, balancing along gables as easily as if I was down on solid ground.

The fresh air helps calm my mind. It smells like rain. I better get this done soon so I get home before the roofs are too wet to be safe. Even I have limits. To have a good footing on wet tiles, I'd have to shift, but I can't do that in daylight. People might raise an eyebrow at a human running on rooftops, but if they saw a panther... well, it wouldn't end well.

My mark lives quite a distance away from the Meow headquarters and by the time I get there, I feel a lot more like myself. This is routine. Something I'm used to. I know how to act in this situation. Now all I have to do is scout the area, see if anyone else is in the house and then do the kill. Easy. I lick my lips as my panther rises to the surface. Maybe I'll be a little more violent than planned.

I crouch down on the roof opposite my mark's house, extending my senses. Only one person in the house, so the chances it's the man I want to kill are high. Even if it's someone else… I'm in the kind of mood that doesn't leave survivors. Killing is a great way to soothe a troubled mind.

When I've made sure everything is as it should be, I step back a bit to give me space. I take a deep breath, then run and jump off the roof – and right onto the house on the other side of the street. Nothing a human could ever do, but luckily, I'm not human. Never have been, never wanted to be. Despite all the hardship my shifter nature gave me, I wouldn't give it up. And if I had to choose, I'd decide to be a panther, not a human.

The roof is in a bad state and I have a hard time keeping tiles from slipping beneath my feet. Going back to solid ground it is. I don't want to alert my mark by strange noises on his ceiling. With a backflip, I vault myself off the roof until I land on all fours in the small garden. Daisies sprinkle the grass and their smell fills my nostrils. I smile. Another thing that most humans will never experience. The fragrant smell of daisies.

There are noises on the other side of the house, giving me the confidence to stand up tall and pick the lock of the back door. It's an old, rusty lock that gives way without much encouragement. The door opens with a slight squeak that even I can't suppress. Oh well. If the man hears it, I'll just have to confront him face to face. I'd actually prefer that. A bit of combat, panicked yelling, then a well-aimed kick at his throat. Or a knife between the ribs. I chuckle when I realise how bloodthirsty I am. All this investigating has left me craving for blood.

"Hello?" a deep voice calls. Yes, he must have heard the door. Hurray. This is far more exciting than sneaking up on him only to cut his throat in a quick, boring move.

I hurry towards the sound. He's in the kitchen, holding a large bread knife. Fun. He's making it a challenge.

I grin wolfishly and pull two daggers from my belt, lazily flipping them in my hands. His eyes widen.

"Are you here to kill me?" he asks, gripping his knife a little harder. His knuckles are turning white and I can smell sweat appearing on his skin. Pathetic.

I give him a saucy wink. "Yes. I'm your angel of death."

His eyes widen. "Who are you working for? I have money. I'll pay double what they did."

Usually, I might consider this, but not today. I'm not here for money. I'm here for sport.

"Time to die," I say dramatically and approach him with the elegance of a predator. Every muscle's movement is carefully controlled. Adrenaline fills me; enough to make me alert, but not enough to make me lose control.

"Please, don't," he begs, stumbling backwards, but the counter stops him from retreating further. He does a few helpless stabs with the knife, clearly showing that he's never held a weapon in all his life. Too easy. I'd hoped he'd at least know how to hold a knife.

I launch forward, nipping his cheek with my dagger, easily evading his knife. I jump back, letting him realise how I could have killed him but didn't. He touches his cheek, leaving his fingers stained with blood.

"Please," he repeats, his voice whiny and pathetic.

I attack again, this time cutting his other cheek. He cries out in panic and pain. This is fun. Playing with prey. Again and again, I strike at him until his body is littered with bleeding gashes. Not enough to kill him, but enough to make me happy.

Someone enters the house through the backdoor. I sniff the air without giving away to the mark that he might be in luck. I grin when I smell a familiar scent. Then frown. What is Lennox doing here?

"Are you quite done yet?" he asks as soon as he enters the kitchen. "I could hear the screams from miles away."

I shrug. "There are still a few places I haven't hurt him yet. Why are you here?"

The man gapes at Lennox, realising that there's no chance of rescue.

"You weren't home, so I followed your tracks. We need to talk."

I sigh. "I've told you I'm not interested in turning detective again. And I'm not going against the Pack either."

"It's not that. It's something personal."

That has me turn around. "Personal?"

Lennox isn't someone who ever opens up about his

feelings. I know him well enough to read him, to know when he's upset, but most people would never be able to tell.

My mark makes a desperate dash for escape, but I throw a knife at him without even looking. From the gurgled squelching sound I assume that it hit its target. His body crumples to the ground.

"You interrupted my work," I complain to Lennox.

He chuckles. "It looked more like fun than work. Has anyone ever told you not to play with your food?"

I grin at him. "You may have mentioned that a couple of times when we were younger. And then did it yourself." I open the fridge and take out a bottle of orange juice. Killing always makes me thirsty. I find some ice cream in the freezer as well, which Lennox immediately takes off me.

I sit on the kitchen island, sipping my juice.

"What's so important that you had to disturb me?" I ask, intrigue filling my mind. There has to be a good reason. Assassins never interfere with each other's work unless it's important. It's a sort of unwritten code.

"We need to talk."

I groan. "We're talking now."

He nods towards the corpse. "You want to do this here, with him around?"

"It's not like he's going to hear whatever secrets you have to tell me."

Lennox chuckles. "You're right." He sighs. "I'm having a problem with my wolf."

I'm used to Lennox talking about his shifted form as if it's separate from his human. He seems to have a different relationship with it than I have with my panther. We're one, I just turn a little more feral when I'm shifted. He almost has two personalities that live in the same body. I have to admit that it creeps me out a tiny bit, but by now, I'm used to it.

"What kind of problem? Just spit it out."

Lennox averts his eyes. Is he embarrassed? That's a first.

"He… he… "

I growl at him.

"He's claimed someone." He says it so fast that I almost don't understand. My heart starts beating faster when the words hit home. Lennox explained it to me long ago. Wolf shifters mate for life, and it's not the human part of them that decides who with. While Lennox could try and resist his wolf, be in a relationship with someone else, his wolf would never stop aching for his mate. Some shifters go crazy when they refuse their wolf.

"I don't know what to do," Lennox admits quietly. "I'm not ready. I don't want to commit to someone I may not even know. But the craving is strong. It fills my thoughts night and day and resisting it is getting harder. I don't know how much longer I'll be able to withstand it."

"Who is it?" I ask, almost dreading the answer. The reason is something I don't want to think about.

"I don't know. I'd have to shift to find out, but I don't want to. What if it's a horrible person? What if it's someone in the Pack? Or someone twice as old as me? There have even been cases of adult wolves claiming a child and then having to wait for a decade until they could actually be with their mate."

"What do you need me to do?" There's a reason he came to me with this. And to be honest, I'm flattered that he still trusts me enough to tell me, even after being apart for so many years. It's like we were never apart.

"I want you to be with me when I shift. Follow me so you can see who my wolf claims. If it's someone you think is bad for me, you need to pull me away, stop me. I've heard stories of our wolves going into a lovesick frenzy when they first meet their mate. I don't want that to happen to me. You need to keep me sane."

I nod. "I'll do my best, but let me warn you, I may think of someone as not suitable that you might end up loving."

He shudders. "I don't think I could love anyone. I'm too busy for love. Too damaged." He whispers the last bit. I want to reach out, hug him, tell him that I'm the same, but I don't do touchy-feely.

"When do you want to do it?" I ask.

"Tonight, after dark. I want to get rid of this feeling as soon as possible."

"But what if it's your soulmate? If you fall in love at first sight? Will you be alright with that?"

He shakes his head. "I don't even want to consider that. I hate how helpless this makes me. How my wolf is taking control and I can't do anything about it. I should be free to decide who I love, right? Nobody should take that decision from me, not even my wolf."

"I agree. I'm glad it doesn't work that way for cats. But then, can you imagine a cat being with just one partner for the rest of her life?" I chuckle. "There's little chance of that."

A tiny frown appears on his forehead, but it's gone before I can think on it.

"Do you think you'll ever settle down?" he asks me.

I shrug. "Maybe. Not really thought about that. I can't really imagine living in a house with a husband, having a mundane life."

"Who says it would have to be mundane?"

I laugh. "I doubt I'd be with an assassin or someone else in my line of work. Have you seen us? We don't settle down. We don't fall in love. I've never seen an assassin couple and I doubt I'll ever will."

Lennox smiles but it seems forced. "You're right. We're not made for love. Sadly, my wolf thinks otherwise. But maybe he'll decide differently tonight. Maybe he'll reconsider when he sees whatever terrible woman he's chosen. Maybe he'll come to his senses."

I take a sip of juice, for once unwilling to tell the truth. I know he's deluding himself, but I don't want him to feel unhappy either.

Whatever happens, I'll help him through it. He's my oldest friend and I'm quite enjoying having him back.

CHAPTER FOUR

Night falls quickly, covering the town in shades of blue. It's a Friday night, so all the streets are busy with people hoping to forget the stress and troubles of the working week. I can smell the alcohol all around me, still fresh but about to turn stale. In an hour or two, the first drunks will stumble along the streets, not sure whether they should return home or go back to the pub for another drink.

Lennox and I head to the outskirts of town, hoping that his mate will not be in the centre of the city where everyone could see him. I doubt he'll have himself fully under control once he shifts today. It's a bit scary, especially because I will have to shift too to keep him in check. A wolf running across town might be just about explainable, but a giant black cat... not so much. There'd be panic and the Pack would certainly get wind of it. I don't want them to remember that I exist.

"Ready?" I ask Lennox, even though I know that he isn't. I can hear his heartbeat drumming faster than it should. He's anxious, more anxious than I've ever seen him.

He shrugs. "Let's do this. Better to know than to fight the urge for the rest of my life. But promise me you'll drag me away if my mate isn't suitable?"

I put one hand on my chest, wiggling my fingers. "Shifter promise."

He chuckles, probably remembering the time when we came up with that oath.

"Good. You're larger than me, you'll be able to stop me. Don't take it personal if I fight back." He grins sheepishly. "My wolf likes to play."

"So do I. And don't worry, I've been longing for a challenge like this, especially since you interrupted my killing earlier."

He takes a deep breath and his heartbeat accelerates further. I can't believe we're about to do this. Somehow, I never imagined either of us having a mate. Occasional lovers, yes, but nothing permanent. Now it's about to change, and it makes me feel something that I can't quite identify. Sadness? Jealousy? Longing? I push it away. I need to focus. Lennox needs me.

He meets my eyes. I don't like what I see in them. He's scared, and I don't like him being scared. He never shows his fear, he never shows any emotion. Especially not something that could be interpreted as weakness.

"Shift," I tell him and let myself fall into my cat form, purring as soon as I'm on all fours. I stretch my back and extend my claws a couple of times. So good. Now to take a nap...

Lennox whines. His beautiful white wolf is twitching

on the ground. I jump to his side, nudging his flank with my head. I wish I could talk to him, but we're different species, even though we're both shifters. All I can do is try and read his body language.

He seems agitated and in pain, rolling around the grass, yelping occasionally. I'd expected him to run to whoever his mate is. This is scaring me.

"What can I do?" I ask in panic, even though I know he can't understand me.

He whines again, then gets to all fours for just long enough to take a step back, away from my touch. The pain of rejection runs through me. He doesn't want my help. Why isn't he letting me take some of his hurt? He's suffering and there's nothing I can do about it.

I purr to show him that I want to help and approach him again, this time not quite touching him. Maybe the touch was uncomfortable for him. Maybe his wolf will only tolerate the touch of his mate just now.

Suddenly, he shifts back, but instead of wearing clothes like he usually would, he's naked. He's curled up on the ground, clutching his legs to his chest.

I don't know what to do. He's vulnerable, terribly vulnerable, and I hate it. I want to protect him, but I also don't want him to feel like he needs protection. He's a proud man and an even prouder wolf.

Instead of shifting too, I lay down, close enough for him to touch me if he wants to, but far enough to give him space. I want him to know that I'm there for him, that I won't leave, no matter what's happened.

Maybe he doesn't have a mate? Maybe something went wrong?

I start purring. It always soothes me when a cat does that, so maybe it works the same for him.

I listen to his heartbeat, fast and shallow. His breathing is too fast.

We lie like that for ages. Him curled up into a ball, naked, suffering. Me, shifted, purring, also suffering.

"We need to talk," he whispers. "Can you shift back?"

Finally. I thought he'd never tell me. I jump to my feet and shift in one fluid motion, being completely human by the time I'm fully standing. As always, I'm wearing the same clothes I did before I shifted, making me very aware of his nakedness. I've never heard of this happening. Even as shifters, our unique magic always makes us keep our clothes.

"What's wrong?" I ask softly, surprising myself. I'm not a soft person.

He sits up, exposing his nakedness. I try not to notice how perfect his body is. How his muscles are sculpting his chest into hard planes, how the thin line of dark hair running down from his belly button points to…

He's hard. Big. Very hard.

Oh my.

He crosses his legs and puts his hands in his lap, almost managing to hide his erection. Seeing his discomfort, I take off my jacket and hand it to him. Without meeting my eyes, he takes it and puts it on his lap like a blanket. Suitably covered, his heartbeat slows down a tiny bit, but he's still nervous.

"What's wrong?" I repeat. "Talk to me."

"I can fight it," he mutters. "I don't have to give in to my wolf."

"So you found out who your mate is?" I ask excitedly. "I wasn't sure if you had."

He laughs harshly. "I did. He showed me right away. I just don't know what to think of it. Or how to tell you."

"Just spit it out. That's usually easiest," I quip, hiding the growing tension I feel.

He finally looks at me, his eyes meeting mine. They're full of emotions and unspoken words. He's trying to tell me through this look alone, but I don't understand.

"He showed me my mate. She's right in front of me."

My heart explodes.

And then I do the stupidest thing ever. I start laughing. Hysterical laughter bubbles from my throat and I press my hands on my mouth, trying to stop that traitorous sound from escaping. It's no use. I laugh and laugh until I need to stop to breathe.

He grimaces. "I didn't expect that response."

I try to stop, I really do, but the laughter just keeps coming.

He gets up, no longer looking at me, and shifts. His white wolf is a light in the dark, a beautiful sight that runs away from me as fast as he can.

He could have thrown a knife at me and it wouldn't have hurt as much.

I get up, a little unsteady on my feet. I should stay

here. Let him go. Mull it over. But no, I crouch down, shift, and run after him.

AT THE BEGINNING, I TRACK HIM BY HIS SCENT, BUT AFTER a while, I realise where he's going. It's no surprise, really. He always used to go there when we were kids. His hidey-hole, his sanctuary. It took him years to take me there for the first time. Even as a child, I understood the significance of that gesture. He'd arrived at the Pack before me, and until I became his friend, he'd been on his own. I had been an outcast because I was a different species from everyone else, he was an outcast because he chose to be.

Even at a sprint, it takes ten minutes to leave the town and head towards the little stone bridge spanning the river. It's old and crumbling in places, but it's clung to life for so long that I doubt it will ever collapse.

I sniff the air before I approach. He's here.

What am I going to say? I don't have any words. No explanations, no words for the emotions raging inside me. I'm so confused and I bet he is too. Neither of us expected this.

He's my friend, not my lover. Definitely not my mate. Yes, I know him better than I know myself, and yes, he's gorgeous, and yes, he would be a better partner than any man I've been with. But... he's Lennox. My friend Lennox. If we cross the line of friendship, there may be no return from it. I've only just found him again, I don't want to lose him over something as silly as love.

Wait, did I think love? Like, being in love? I must be confused. I've never been in love. I'm an assassin, I'm incapable of it. I couldn't do my job otherwise.

I start purring to make him aware of my presence. He likely already knows, but I want him to be able to stop me in case he wants to be alone. I'm not sure I'd leave if he asked me to. We need to sort this out.

Just as predicted, he's in a hollow under the bridge. I can't believe our old mattress is still here. It's stained and covered in dirt, but even from here, I can smell our scents on it. We used to spend a lot of time here. We'd try to complete our assignments as quickly as possible so we could hang out here without our Pack masters missing us. I spent some of the happiest moments of my childhood down here under the bridge. We made it ours, added some decoration to the bridge walls, carved out more of thc hollow when we got too big to fit into it.

And now, Lennox is on that old mattress, human, naked, vulnerable.

I slowly walk towards him, half expecting him to turn and run again. Or to tell me to fuck off. I'd understand. I was an idiot, laughing like that. It must have hurt him. I wish I could take it back.

I never stop purring as I lay down by his side, my fur touching his naked skin. I snuggle against him but stay shifted. This way, there won't be a conversation. No words that could hurt. Just companionship. Showing him how much I care. How much I like him.

After a moment, he wraps his arms around me, his fingers curling into my thick fur. He lays his head onto my back and I can feel his breath growing slower. His human heartbeat synchronises with mine until we're merged by touch and sound.

Now, I almost wish I could talk to him, but I don't want to interrupt this moment of closeness by shifting. So I continue purring gently, enjoying the feeling of him touching me.

We lie like that for ages. His shifter nature is keeping him warm, aided by my own body warmth. His nakedness no longer bothers me.

"Thank you for coming here," he whispers suddenly, startling me. My purring stops as I listen, waiting for him to say more, but he stays quiet. I extend a paw, careful to keep my claws in, and wrap it around his back. I don't use my full weight; I don't want to hurt him. He's so vulnerable right now, emotionally and physically.

"I can still feel it," he mutters after a while. "The pull. Even though you're next to me, my wolf still wants to get even closer. It wants you to shift so I can mate with you."

If I were human, I'd blush. Not because of the thought of having sex. It's a natural thing, there's nothing embarrassing about it. No, because of the word 'mate'. It sounds so intimate. Not fucking. Mating. Lovingly bonding. I'm terrified of it.

"I don't want this to change things, but I'm not sure if I can fight against the urge forever. Maybe it's better if I leave town. It might be easier if we're far apart. The distance might take the edge off."

I shift before I can stop myself. I've never shifted

while lying on the ground before, but I no longer have control over my body. The thought of him leaving…

"You're naked," he whispers, a barely audible chuckle hiding between his words.

"I am," I say, stating the obvious. This is the first time I've ever shifted without clothes before. I hope this is a one-time thing. It would be terribly inconvenient. I'd become known as the naked assassin.

"Are you okay with it?" he whispers, his eyes meeting mine.

Strangely enough, I am. All doubt has fled my mind. It feels right, his naked skin on mine, his breath entangling with my own.

I inch closer to him until our lips are close enough to touch. Just a tiny move, but who's going to do it? Is this right? Moments ago, Lennox was talking about resisting the pull of his mating bond, now we're entwined, naked, our hearts beating fast. I think I can feel the bond too. Faint, but growing. Or maybe it's my own heart telling me what I should have known before.

"There will be no return from this," Lennox whispers, his breath hot against my lips.

"I know," I reply, my voice shaking. "Are you sure this isn't just your wolf? If we do this, I need all of you. Both of you."

CHAPTER FIVE

"I've wanted to do this ever since I saw you outside that house," he whispers.

I chuckle. "You mean since you poisoned me."

It's strange to be having a conversation while our lips are a hair's width apart. It would be so easy to kiss him, but yet it's so hard at the same time. I'd have to jump over my own shadow, break through the barriers I've built and maintained for so long. When I'm with men, I never kiss them. We fuck, we never see each other again. No feelings, no attachments. Nothing but satisfying the physical itch. I'm a grown woman, I have needs. Luckily, there are lots of men feeling the same way.

With Lennox, it's different. With him, there'd be a morning after. Having to talk about it. Having to analyse my feelings. I don't think I'm ready for it.

"Lennox," I mutter, but then his lips are on mine and all doubt flees my mind. His lips are soft and his kiss is gentle, almost cautious. As if he's afraid that I might pull back. And yes, I'm tempted. My mind is screaming at me to get up and run. This is such a bad idea. Yet his lips… I kiss him back, opening myself to his probing tongue, letting him in. I've never kissed like this before. There's never been emotion involved. With every swipe of his tongue, every touch of his lips on mine, I feel myself getting closer to him.

I let my body have free reign. Let it move as it wants to. I push back the doubt, the uproar in my mind, concentrating instead on how good it feels. How he's made for me.

It's one of the hardest things I've ever done. Giving up control. Ignoring my rational mind. Relaxing, simply enjoying the moment. All of my instincts are fighting me.

His hands wander over my body, gently exploring me. We've been friends for so long, but never been this close. It's too late to go back now. So I do the only thing I can: go with the flow.

I end up on top of him, straddling his hips. His hands worship my breasts, leaving me breathless and gasping. Others might call it a moan, but cats don't moan. We might make sounds of pleasure, but not moans. That's for humans who don't have control of their bodies. I can resist-

He slips a finger between my lips and I moan, arching my back, coming undone.

What is this man doing to me?

I'm afraid that he's breaking barriers that should have stayed untouched.

As we cling to each other, merging in new ways, I try to ignore the feeling that I made a massive mistake.

❀ ❀ ❀ ❀ ❀ ❀

WE STAY TOGETHER ALL NIGHT, OUR BODIES TANGLED, one ending where the other begins. I'm itching to get up and run away. It's what I always do when I've had sex with a guy. This is the first time I've stayed. Even slept a little, albeit brief and restless. His arm was around my shoulders and I couldn't relax with him touching me. I'm not used to being touched. It's both disturbing and beautiful.

I wish I were a normal woman. And he a normal guy. Two humans who could love each other. Who don't have baggage that makes it impossible for them to be together.

I can't do it anymore. I move as slowly as possible, leaving his embrace. I'm sure he knows what I'm doing; the way his breathing has changed means he's awake. He lets me go though. I shift and run as fast as I can, ignoring the pain in my chest that gets worse the further I get away from him.

By the time I get home, my head is slightly clearer, but my chest still aches. Is that a side effect of being his wolf's mate? Or am I somehow imagining this pain? Either way, it's annoying.

"Look what the cat's dragged in," Beth snickers, surprising me as I walk into the kitchen. Oh my, I really need to focus. Nobody ever manages to sneak up on me like that. Never. Beth seems to come to the same conclusion and looks at me quizzically.

"Are you ill?" she asks while popping a handful of crisps into her mouth.

"No, just tired," I mutter and put the kettle on. Tea will cure all my woes, right? That's what they say. Tea is a miracle cure for some completely unscientific reason. Let's hope it works. I can't do my job when I'm feeling like this.

"Maybe you should take a break," Beth says, chewing loudly. "Lily's going to that convention thingy, why not join her? You could do with a holiday."

The way she's all nice and helpful makes me suspicious. "So that you can take over the house while we're gone? Invite all your boyfriends and have some kind of poison party?"

"Not poisons," she quips. "Body parts, more likely. I've got that new friend who works in the morgue, lovely guy. Of course, he thinks I'm a timid, innocent girl who's scared of dead people and simply wanted the keys to the morgue as a dare."

I snicker. "Of course. When are you going to show him that you're not exactly innocent?"

She shrugs. "Who knows. Let's see how he is in bed. Maybe he thinks I'm too innocent to want that, so in that case, I might have to intervene."

I pour myself a cup of tea while I listen to her prattling on about that morgue guy. That's how I used to do it. Have some fun with a guy, then drop him. No commitment, no attachment.

"... by the way, the cat has returned."

I stare at her, lost in where our conversation has gone.

"Ryker?"

She nods. "He's in the backyard as always. Didn't

want to come in. I gave him some snacks but he refused to eat. I guess the whole 'you're a shifter' reveal didn't go too well?"

I sigh. "You could say that. And I've done entirely too much peopling today. I'm going to bed."

Ignoring her laughter, I head upstairs. I don't feel guilty for ignoring Ryker. It was him who ran away after all. Now he can wait, especially after returning sooner than I'd thought. I need some time on my own.

MY ATTIC IS NICE AND QUIET. I OPEN THE WINDOW, THEN climb onto my hammock, shoes and all. I couldn't care less. I just want to rest. I got some sleep while with Lennox, but-

No. I won't go there. No more men. Just me. Kat. A lone hunter. An assassin without emotions. A killer, trained to murder people without regrets. That's me. Not this strange woman who doesn't know how to react to the men around her. That's not me, not in the slightest. She's weak, she's confused.

In a way, I wish I hadn't met Lennox. Not for a second time, I mean. I treasured the memories I have of us as children, but now that we're both grown up, it's getting complicated.

I close my eyes, but sleep won't come. My mind is too busy trying to make sense of everything. I've dealt with dangerous situations, but none of them has ever threatened my heart. My sense of identity.

Maybe I should follow Lily's example and go on

holiday. Leave the town, leave all the problems behind. Sounds like a great idea, except that I've never been further away than five miles down the road, and that I'd miss my job. I've tried going cold turkey - cold cat? - before. It doesn't work. After two days without killing, I get antsy. It's in my nature to be a predator. I can't just shut it off.

But what the fuck am I going to do now?

For the first time in my life, I don't have an answer to that.

CHAPTER SIX

At some point, I must have fallen asleep. I'm curled up in my hammock, blinking at the afternoon sun streaming through the window.

Sounds from downstairs tell me that at least two other people are around. Probably Beth and Benjamin. Lily must be gone by now, enjoying her holiday. Pah. Not jealous at all.

I get up and stretch, purring as my back curves in the most delicious way. I'm tempted to shift just so I can feel the sensation of my claws extending, but that would be a waste of energy. I shifted too often in the past twenty-four hours and my body needs a break. It will get painful otherwise.

I undress, deciding that I've been in the same clothes for too long. I very rarely sweat, but my clothes tend to get dirty fast from climbing up walls and running over rooftops.

Once naked, I stretch again. Nice, that feels even better.

Meow.

Luckily, I hear the cat approach before it appears in front of my attic window. I groan and quickly grab a towel from the floor, wrapping it around me. I don't like other people seeing me naked. I may be confident in everything else, but nakedness is one thing I can't stand. Except with Lennox, apparently.

Ryker's furry face looks through the window just when I'm covered. I thought he was going to be away for a bit. Why is he back now? Has he decided to tell me the truth, that he's been a shifter all his life and just made fun of me? Nah, I saw how shocked he was. It wasn't a prank, no matter how much I wanted it.

With a sigh, I open the window. Ryker jumps in with an elegant pounce, landing with his head held high. Such a show-off. He probably doesn't even realise he does it. The arrogance of cats. Hadn't I grown up in the Pack, I might be the same, but they made sure none of us got too arrogant. Confident, proud in our abilities, yes, but not arrogant.

"Why are you here?" I ask, not even trying to be polite.

He meows again, his voice urgent. He's worried, no, afraid.

Fuck. I'd not planned to shift for the rest of the day, but the fear in his eyes makes me reconsider. He's not here because he's a shifter. Something must have happened.

"Turn around," I tell him. He looks at me quizzically but does as I say. I drop the towel and shift.

It hurts like hell. I cry out in pain as my bones elongate and fur erupts from my skin. My gums bleed as my teeth change, filling my mouth with the sharp taste of iron. My nails lengthen into claws, and right now, I know why pulling out fingernails is a great torture method.

I don't think it's ever been that painful.

By the time the shift is over, I'm curled up on the floor, my tail quivering, my body still getting used to the extra appendage.

"I'm sorry," Ryker says softly. "I wouldn't have come if I'd had a choice."

Slowly, I sit up, leaning on my forelegs like a sphynx. Without the human head. Partial shifts only allow me to lengthen my fingernails as a human, but that's as far as it goes. Some people at the Pack were able to do proper partial shifts, having some limbs human and others animal. Not me, though.

"What's wrong?" I groan, my tongue swiping over my sharp teeth. I feel like drinking a bucket full of milk to get rid of the taste of blood. I like to taste other people's blood, but not my own. That feels like cannibalism.

"Haru and Mila are dead. Pumpkin is gone. Five other kittens are missing." He blinks at me, his eyes full of fear. "I don't know what to do."

"Wait, start from the beginning. What happened?"

"I came back to our den. Haru and Mila had been in charge of looking after the kittens; they like to get up to all sorts of shenanigans. I grounded Pumpkin because he'd broken into our food stores last night, so he would have been with them. He's a bit too old to stay there usually, but…"

He stares at me in desperation. "He's my son. Please, help me find them. The cats are in uproar, most of them are scared. Nobody has ever infiltrated our home. All of us have escaped awful pasts, and the den has been a place of safety. Until now."

"Of course I'll help. Do you know if it was humans? Other shifters?"

"Haru and Mila were stabbed with a knife, that's all I know. There were no scents at all. No traces. It's like they appeared out of thin air, took the kittens and disappeared again."

"That's impossible, there must be some sort of evidence. Nobody can simply vanish without a trace."

"Don't you think I haven't checked?" Ryker snaps. "You're welcome to look and see for yourself. That's why I came here. You're an assassin, you know how to move unseen. Maybe you can spot something I haven't." His voice broke. "Please. It's my son."

I get up to all fours, ignoring how my legs are a little shaky. I won't be able to shift back for some time, not without ending up being incapacitated. I extend my senses to check on Benjamin's kittens. If someone is kidnapping baby cats, they could be in danger too, but no, they're all in the room he's turned into his personal cat paradise.

"Let me tell the others before we go," I say, slowly walking towards the window. I feel like I've run a marathon, then got drunk, then ran another marathon while wearing stilts.

"Are you alright?" he asks and I put some more effort into the way I walk. I don't want him to think me weak.

"Too many shifts in the past twenty-four hours," I explain. "I'll have to stay like this for a while."

"Then how are you going to talk to your humans?"

I snicker, almost hearing the unspoken 'pets' at the end of his sentence. Most cats don't understand why I bother with humans. They don't understand that half of me is human, too, and that two-legged people can come in handy occasionally. Beth and Benjamin are some excellent examples of useful humans.

"I have my ways," I reply and jump out of the open window, climbing onto the overhanging roof. My muscles complain loudly, but I ignore the pain. It will get better the more I move − hopefully.

Running over the roof and to the other side of the house, I jump down onto the wall surrounding our backyard, and then land on the ground. I think a few of my bones are close to shattering. I've been wanting to find a way to change the ladder leading down from my loft so that I can use it in my panther form, but there have always been other priorities.

Luckily, the back door has been left open − I'll have to chastise the others for that later − and we sneak in. I can smell Beth in the living room. She doesn't look up from her book when we enter. *100 Deadly Poisons and How to Make Them*. Nice. I will have to borrow that later. Sounds like the perfect bedtime read.

I bump against her knee and growl a little, making it very clear that I need her attention. She glowers at me.

"I'm busy."

"Get up and get the board." To her, that must sound like a series of loud, intimidating growls.

"I love it when you speak cat to me," she chuckles, but she does heave herself off the sofa and grabs our whiteboard from the cupboard. She lays it on the carpet in front of me and I lift a paw, letting her attach a velcro strap to it. It looks ridiculous, but we've discovered that's the only way I can use a pen while shifted.

Bethany clips a large marker pen to my velcro brace and I start scribbling away. Even I have trouble reading the result, but luckily Beth is used to my paw-writing.

LENNOX

"You want me to get Lennox?" she asks. "Why don't you just do it yourself?"

I growl and nod towards Ryker, who's watching us with growing impatience.

"Okay, okay, I'll get him. Where shall I send him?"

I turn to Ryker. "Where's the den?"

"Do you really trust the dog? I've never told an outsider about our location."

I sigh. "Lennox is the best tracker I know. If anyone can find the kittens, it's him."

It's painful to admit that Lennox is better at tracking than me. At least I'm better at killing, much better. Only Gryphon gets close to my level of skill.

"It's in the abandoned chocolate factory. Their solar-powered heating still works, so it's the perfect hideout in the winter."

CHOC FAC

"Chocolate face? Faeces?" Bethany grins as if she's

proud of that joke. "Chocolate… factory? But that's one been closed for years."

Ryker groans. "Is she always that slow?"

"She must be tired," I reply, feeling like I need to apologise for Bethany for some reason. I guess she's part of my team, and I need my team to look good. We have a reputation to lose.

"Shall I come too?" Beth asks.

I draw a tick on the board. The more investigators, the better. She won't be able to help with tracking, but she might be able to come in handy with other things. I want to solve this as fast as possible. I've come to like little Pumpkin, and the thought of him and other kittens being in danger tears at my heartstrings. And Mila… I don't want to think of her as dead. Shara must be heartbroken. The two of them seemed to be really in love, judging from the heavy making out session I interrupted not long ago.

I never had much to do with Haru, but I remember him because he looked like an exact copy of myself, just a lot smaller.

"How's Shara holding up?" I ask Ryker.

"She's run away. Not sure if she'll return. Her and Mila were planning to adopt a kitten soon…"

He looks at the ground, hiding his expression. Poor him. Two of his friends dead, his son and other kittens missing. No wonder Ryker is emotional.

I write FAST on the board, then hold out my paw for Bethany to remove the velcro brace.

"Alright, I'll get Lennox and will meet you there. Will you shift then and explain what's going on?"

I shake my head. I won't be able to. Maybe tonight, but not until then. Which is a slight problem. I'm going to have to get to the chocolate factory without being seen. It's the middle of the day and there will be people all over the place. Humans who wouldn't understand a panther running through the streets. We'll have to stick to the roofs, but I know there are some stretches on the way where there aren't any houses lining the road. Well, I'll just have to be careful. And fast. My muscles groan in protest at that.

"Suit yourself." She drops her book on the table – I make a mental note to steal it later - and leaves the room with a yawn. Hopefully, she's noticed that time is of the essence.

I give Ryker a nod and we run out of the house, up onto the roof and towards the industrial part of town. We've got kittens to save.

CHAPTER SEVEN

I'm in agony, but I'm trying hard not to show it. Reaching the last few houses before a long stretch of empty grassland is a relief. Jumping from roof to roof isn't good for my aching body. I feel twenty years older than I am. No, make that thirty.

To distract myself from the pain, I let Ryker catch up with me until we're running side by side. He must have trouble keeping up, being so much smaller than me, but he doesn't complain.

"How many cats are there?" I ask him, not for the first time. Before, he always evaded my question, but now, it's essential that I know. If he wants me to investigate this properly, then I need to have all the information.

"Thirty-six," he replies grudgingly. He's out of breath, just like me, but I manage to hide it better. "Thirty-four now that Mila and Haru are gone."

A sombre silence falls between us, interrupted only

by the soft sound of our paws hitting the ground and our ragged breaths exploding from our lungs.

I feel his sadness though, and it makes me want to distract him. Call it me being social. Or nice. Either sounds like a terrible idea.

"Who's Pumpkin's mother?"

Only after asking the question do I realise how that may not have been the right thing to say. I don't need to remind him that Pumpkin is gone, but I've been wondering that for a while now. Especially knowing that he's a shifter. Was his mate a cat? A shifter? It can't have been a human since Ryker doesn't know how to shift. I assume Pumpkin won't have enough shifter genes to make him able to shift, but who knows. It would depend on Ryker's parents and on the female who gave birth to Pumpkin.

He doesn't answer for quite a while. I almost assume that I won't get a response when he clears his throat.

"I don't even know her name. She was a drunk one night stand. I usually don't do that kind of stuff, but things had happened and I needed to forget. Twelve weeks later, another cat brought Pumpkin to me, said his mother had died on an overdose."

"Wait, drunk? Overdose? Are we still talking about cats?"

He laughs darkly. "It seems you're not as cattish as you think. Fermented apples are great for getting drunk. Pumpkin's mother lived with human junkies though, and she regularly managed to lick up some leftovers of their drugs. I think they even put vodka in her bowl occasionally. She was an alcoholic, and the only reason I ever slept with her was that she was there in the right place at the right time. Not that I regret it. Pumpkin is the most amazing kitten."

"That he is," I say, remembering how the little cat first jumped into my life. He's who started it all, my relationship with this strange family of cats. Without him, I might never have solved the Kindler case.

My resolve hardens. We need to find him before he's harmed. And the other kittens. People who hurt children are the worst, whether the children are human, shifter or cats.

"We're going to find him," I tell him, and it's a promise that I intend to keep, no matter what. "And we're going to punish the monsters who took him and the other kittens. We'll make sure Mila and Haru get justice."

"You know he admires you?" Ryker mutters and it takes me a moment to realise that he means Pumpkin.

"He does?"

"You're his hero. He kept saying how he wants to be like Kat when he grows up. Solve crime, help people."

If I could blush, I would. That little kitten totally overestimated my humanity. I only solved the Kindler case because I got paid extremely well for it. And helping people… not if I can avoid it.

It takes so much time and energy. I'm not altruistic, I'm not a hero. I'm an assassin who branched out into investigating a case a single time. Never again. Well, except for this kitten case, but that's different. I know the cats involved. It's personal.

We run on in silence until we finally reach the

abandoned chocolate factory. Its three chimneys reach high into the sky, almost seeming to scratch the clouds. I imagine the clouds purring for a second, then decide to focus on what's important. I can't get distracted.

Ryker leads me through a hole in the wall that's almost too small for me to squeeze through. It unpleasantly ruffles my fur.

"Sorry, I'm the largest of us and I fit," Ryker apologises.

"Are you calling me fat?"

He barks out an involuntary laugh. "No, just big boned."

I snort and for a moment, I forget why we're here. I like Ryker. He's got a wicked sense of humour, he's gorgeous and he's kind. And I'm totally not interested. The only reason I keep him around is because I need his cats, and because I'm curious about how a shifter couldn't know what he was all his life.

Shaking my fur until it aligns in the right way again, I follow Ryker deeper into the factory. Some machinery is still there, strange apparatuses that I don't understand. Once, they made chocolate, now they're just dark shadows in this massive hall. Light streams through a few broken windows, just enough to show the thick layer of dust covering the floor, interspersed only by a path of cat paw prints.

The air is thick with the scent of dozens of cats. They've each marked their territory, but the overwhelming scent is that of Ryker. This is home and he's made sure that everybody knows it.

I sniff the air for any human or shifter scents, but all

I can smell is cats. There are no footprints either, but that doesn't have to mean that there were no humans. I'm sure there are other ways into this place. The factory is huge.

Ryker meows loudly, announcing our presence. I'm sure the other cats knew already, but everyone must be on edge.

Three sets of glowing eyes appear in the shadows to our left. I recognise two of their scents before I see them. Storm and Nyx. The latter has been spending a lot of time at my house, playing with Benjamin, letting him spoil her. Her white fur shimmers in the darkness, while I only see Storm's blue eyes. Storm is black as the night and just as stealthy. She's a great asset, just as much at home in the shadows as I am. She'd make a great assassin, if she was a little bigger and had hands to carry weapons.

I don't recognise the third cat, but there must be a lot of cats in here who I've not met before. Only some of them came to my headquarters to collect their reward.

"What's the situation?" Ryker asks, his voice calm, but I can feel the tension rippling through his body.

"Nothing's changed," Storm replies. "We've not been able to find anything that would give us a lead on what happened to the babies. Let's see if the half-cat can do any better." She regards me with an arrogant look.

"Half-cat?" I'm kind of offended. I like to consider myself as a full cat when I'm shifted, and a three-quarter-human when I'm not. A human with feline benefits.

"That's what they call you," Ryker explains quietly. "Nyx, two of the other people who work with Kat will arrive soon. Wait for them outside and lead them here."

"More two-leggers?" the third cat asks, a male with a hoarse voice. "Isn't one enough already?"

He's a tabby with patchy stripes, looking rather ordinary. A cat you wouldn't give a second look out in the street, unlike Nyx or Ryker.

"They're part of my team," I say sharply. "If you don't want my help, say it now."

His spine arches for a moment, then he backs down, coming to his senses before I have to give him a lesson in respecting his betters. I really don't have time to exult my dominance over Ryker's cats. They better just do what I say.

"Show me where they were taken," I ask Ryker.

He nods gravely and leads me on through another hole in a wall. "We've split our home into several areas. One for storage of supplies, one for the older cats who need some support, a nursery for the kittens, and a few other rooms for us adult cats. Mila was killed outside the nursery, Haru inside. They were trying to defend the kittens…"

I can almost see the sadness pouring from him. He's trying to keep it together, but cracks are appearing in his armour, letting his emotions leak out.

We walk through a room filled with cats, all of them brimming with anxiety and worry. They stare at us, some of them without a spark of hope. They've already given up. It makes me angry. We're going to find those kittens. There's no alternative. And it won't be of any help to have a bunch of sad cats around us.

Before we even get to the nursery, Shara's cries shatter the silence. I don't think I've ever heard a cat make these kinds of sounds. Grief, heartbreak, pain.

We round a corner, now entering a corridor that would have once housed offices. Shara is on the floor, wrapped around Mila's lifeless body. Her moans echo off the metal walls, amplifying her sorrow. Poor thing. She was in love with Mila. The first lesbian cats I ever came across. They were so cute together, but now one of them is dead and the other heartbroken.

Anger fills me. This isn't right. I'm going to find whoever did this and then kill them slowly, painfully. Rip out their fingernails one by one. Pull out their teeth until they're shaking with pain. Draw lines on their skin with my sharpest knives. They're going to suffer, just like Shara is suffering.

I don't try to talk to her. I know she doesn't care about anything besides her grief just now. Later, I will somehow have to get her to leave Mila's body so that I can examine it, but that's for then, not now.

Behind them is a wooden door with a large crack at the bottom. Large enough for cats to squeeze through, but definitely too small for me. I sigh and get up on my hind legs, pressing down the door handle. Luckily, it's not locked and opens with a click.

Inside, it's carnage. The remains of cushions and blankets are all over the floor, covered in feathers and scraps of fabric. Blood splatters paint the walls to our right, glaring down at Haru's corpse. He's covered in blood, his fur drenched with it.

My anger turns into fury. I slowly approach him, sniffing the air for any unusual scents. There's a strange one hidden behind the smell of cats and cat urine (some of the kittens must have been too young to have full control over their bladder). It's faint, hard to focus on, but it's there, just about. It's familiar, but I don't recognise it, or at least I can't name it. Like a scent from long ago, buried in my memory.

Haru is on his side, his eyes closed, his claws fully extended. They're caked in blood. He must have fought for his life, for the life of the kittens. I'll have Beth take a sample to test for DNA. Hopefully, it isn't all his own blood. We don't have a DNA database to test it against, but it would tell us if it was a human or shifter who did this. And maybe I can get Benjamin to break into the police headquarters again and access their lab. No, not maybe. I'll simply order him to. Sometimes, I'm still getting used to the whole Kat-is-a-business-owner-with-employees.

I'd love to shift and examine him with my hands, but I know I can't, not for a while. Despite their size, my paws are able to be delicate when touching things, but I do miss the opposable thumbs. They make my life a lot easier.

I'll wait for Beth and Lennox to do it instead. For now, I walk around the room, taking in the scene. A few toys are strewn across the floor, all of them well used. Empty food bowls line one wall, although some of them have been overturned. By the kittens or the perpetrator?

I keep my nose close to the ground, soaking in every scent I can find. By the time I've circled the room, I've catalogued the scents of the missing kittens. They're easy to separate from the scents of adult cats, which are full of hormones and arrogance. Pumpkin's smell is somewhere in between; a teenager who's slowly starting to come into adulthood. Haru's scent is thick in the air, his blood increasing its potency. Even once his body has been removed, it will be hard to get his scent out of the room.

"Anything?" Ryker asks impatiently once I've circled the nursery a second time.

"There's that scent," I mutter thoughtfully. "It's familiar and yet not. I don't think it's that of a cat, nor that of a human. Something else, something in between."

"A cat shifter?" He sniffs the air. "I can't smell it."

I shake my head. "I doubt it. I don't know of any other cat shifters in this town. And wouldn't you be able to scent them? You can scent me, right?"

"Yes, but your scent is fainter than that of other cats. It's how we recognise you. You smell of humans and a tiny bit of cat."

I'm offended. A *tiny* bit of cat? I'm the biggest cat in the room and I feel just as catty as they do. Maybe even more so. Just look at my massive body, muscular and strong, my silky fur, my sharp claws. I'm a killing machine, a cat perfected by nature.

"Don't you have any siblings?" Ryker asks. "Or parents?"

I hiss at him before I can stop myself. "No," I snap,

making it very clear that this conversation is not going to continue.

He backs off, bowing his head in submission.

Noises in the distance announce Bethany and Lennox. Even though she's better than most humans at walking quietly, she's still making a racket compared to the cats. Lennox earns himself some hisses and growls from Ryker's family. Hopefully, he won't take it personal. Cats and dogs have always been at odds, and even though he's a wolf, that doesn't make much of a difference. It's a miracle him and I became friends. And now, we're... what exactly? Still friends? Fuck buddies? Friends with benefits? Something more?

Urgh. I wish I didn't need him for this, but he's a better tracker than I am, and this is about little Pumpkin and other innocent kittens. I need to put my personal issues aside.

When they enter the room, Beth sucks in a breath at the sight of Haru.

"Poor kitty," she mutters before kneeling beside the body. She puts on some gloves and gently examines the deep cuts, while Lennox walks around the room. He's human, his muscular body confined by clothes. For a second, I regret that he's not naked as I left him, but then shut those thoughts into a deep, dark corner of my mind. I'm not a cat in heat. I'm a professional. I can work with him, no matter what happened between us.

"Kat, what happened?" Lennox asks, probably expecting me to shift and tell him.

"She can't shift," Bethany says before I have to resort to charades. "I think she's overdone it."

Lennox groans. "That may be my fault. Sorry. So, two cats dead, and from the scents in here, I assume there were more cats? That are now dead or missing?"

I nod. If I could, I'd correct him and tell them that they're not dead, that they aren't allowed to be dead, but I'm stuck with nods and headshakes. My body still hurts and shifting now would leave me incapacitated for hours. I don't think I've ever regretted sex this much.

"Kat, do you know the jaguar shifter? Her scent seems familiar."

Jaguar?

I freeze.

Fuck.

I should have recognised it. I'm a jaguar myself, after all, in a way. I prefer to call myself a panther, since I'm all black with no spots, but I know that technically, I'm a jaguar. I dimly remember that my father was a panther and my mother a spotted jaguar. That's pretty much the only thing I remember about them. And now that Lennox has said that…

Yes, I know the scent. I do recognise it. Even though my subconscious has been trying hard for the past few minutes to fool me.

I remember the scent. From long ago, so long that it's been just a faint memory that I almost forgot.

Fuck, fuck, fuck.

I run out of the room, ignoring Ryker's calls, ignoring the cats that jump up as I run past them.

My mother is back. And she's a cat killer.

CHAPTER EIGHT

It's Ryker who finds me curled up into a ball at the edge of a field. I ran until my aching body refused to let me continue. I let myself collapse in the field, knowing that I'd be alone here. Able to think. The sharp stalks pricking my skin echo what's going on in my mind.

Pain. Betrayal. Confusion.

I thought my mother was dead. Otherwise, why would she have left me with the Pack? I wasn't stolen away like most of the other children. I was brought to the Pack, handed to them like a present. I knew my father was dead, I dimly remember him dying. My mother was sick, weak, and I always thought she'd given me to the Pack because she knew that she was dying, that she wasn't going to be able to look after me. That it was the only way for her to know that I'd survive.

That's what I told myself all my life. That she couldn't have returned for me. That she'd died. It's how I got through living with the Pack. Knowing that it had been my mother's last act to bring me there. That she probably hadn't known how bad it was there. Better with the Pack than ending up on the streets. I'd never have survived there as a toddler. I don't know how old I was exactly when she left me, but I can't have been older than three or four. Old enough to have fragments of memories, too young to make it on my own on the streets.

But even worse than the sense of betrayal is my confusion over why my mother would have been at the chocolate factory. Why kill two cats? Why kidnap kittens? It didn't make any sense. I'd thought it might have been humans who wanted the kittens for experimentation or some other evil scheme, or maybe even Pack shifters. But not my mother. Not a cat shifter.

Ryker lies down by my side, his fur touching mine. He doesn't speak. Doesn't move. Just lies there, giving me the comfort of his company. I'm glad he doesn't talk to me. I wouldn't know what to say. I feel like a traitor. Maybe he thinks that I intentionally didn't identify the scent. But then, no, he wouldn't be here if he mistrusted me. He's not come to blame me. He's come to help.

I kind of want to cry, but it's not something I do. Katriona Feln doesn't cry. Maybe I would if I'd been raised by my mother rather than the Pack. In the Pack, every weakness is exploited, so I quickly learned never to show my emotions, until they'd died off, locked away. Tears can be death in places like the Pack.

Night falls and I'm starting to get cold. I have a thick fur, but lying in the same position without moving for hours hasn't been a good idea. I'm stiff and sore. I might be able to shift again soon, but I better do that at home so that I can fall into my hammock and sleep for a long, long time.

"Do you want to go home?" Ryker asks softly, almost as if he's afraid to break the silence.

"Not really," I mutter, my voice hoarse. "But I think it's time."

"Want to talk?"

I don't. But then my mouth opens and words tumble out, without me in control. Damn my brain.

"I didn't know it was my mother. I swear, I didn't recognise her scent. She abandoned me when I was a child..."

Abandoned. There it is. Until now, I've convinced myself that it was for my own good, that she left me to save me. Now, I know that it's not true. She abandoned me. She could have come back, saved me from my life in the Pack, but she didn't. She left me to a life of pain, slavery and abuse. What mother would do that?

"She's not my mother," I say harshly. "She may have borne me, but I don't accept that she's my mother. The mother I remember wouldn't kill. She wouldn't kidnap innocent babies. She wouldn't have left me..."

Fuck. My eyes itch. No, I'm not going to cry.

Remember your training, Kat. Tears are death. Tears are weakness. Don't let Ryker see you like that. He needs to respect you. You're not a weak female who needs to be comforted. You're stronger than him. Stronger than all of them.

I manage to swallow back the tears and my eyes stop itching. Good. That's progress.

I get up and shake my body, trying to get rid of some of the stiffness.

"Let's go home," I say with a sigh and start running.

RYKER FOLLOWS ME ALL THE WAY BACK. I'M NOT SURE why he's doing that. Shouldn't he be out there looking for his son? Instead, he's with me, watching me mope. What a waste of time. And yet, I'm kind of grateful for his presence. He keeps me grounded, even though he's not doing anything besides being there.

I take the route through the backyard, up the bins and then onto the roof, until I'm in the attic. My little sanctuary.

Ryker lands behind me, his soft paws barely making a sound. He's big for a cat, but nowhere near my size. I wonder if one of his parents was a big cat rather than just a domesticated house cat. He looks like he could have a trace of lion blood in him.

With a pained groan, I drop to the floor and let the shift take over. I want to be human again; I prefer to sleep on my hammock rather than as a cat on the floor.

The pain is worse than anticipated. I scream as my fur is peeled off my body, as my bones crack and break. Pain, so much pain. Whimpers break through my gritted teeth. I don't want to scream, don't want the others to know how bad it is, but I can't help it. The pain overwhelms me, grips me tight. My body changes agonisingly slow, making me experience every second of it. I should have stayed a cat. Should have known this was a bad idea.

I'm only half conscious of what goes on around me. Ryker is still there, watching me, but there are other people too. I want to get up, open my eyes and make sure they're not a threat, but I don't find the energy to do so. I'm being tortured by my own body and there's nothing I can do about it but wait until it's over.

"She's bleeding. Get some bandages."

I am? I shouldn't bleed. Sometimes I bite my tongue while shifting, but I doubt they're talking about that. Whoever they are.

The pain is giving way to thick fog, embracing me and carrying me away from the agony that still slides through my bones.

"Has this ever happened before?"

"Should we get Lennox?"

No, not Lennox. I don't want him to see me like this.

I can't move, can't talk, all I can do is scream and whimper. Even though I barely feel any pain anymore, my body is still reacting to it.

I wish I could just black out. Go to sleep and wake up when it's all over. Sadly, my mind has other plans. Keeping me awake, although it's all muddled and not quite real. As if I'm looking at the world through a mirror.

"We need to stop the blood flow. It's getting worse."

Maybe that's why I feel so dreamy. Loss of blood can do that. I take advantage of that regularly when I want information from people. Take enough blood from them and they might get woozy enough to spill their secrets. I'm rather glad that I can't talk just now.

"She's burning up, we need something cold. Do you have any ice?"

So many voices. I can't keep them straight in my head. Can't figure out how many people they are. They keep talking but only a few sentences filter through.

Please, someone knock me out. I don't want to be in this state anymore. Just knock me out and be done with it. Being helpless is the worst thing that could ever happen to me. And right now, I'm as helpless as I've ever been. I hate it. Even at the Pack, even with a collar, I was more in control than I am now.

I try to speak, try to tell them to hit me on the head or strangle me or whatever they want, but I can't even open my mouth. The taste of blood slowly registers, making me want to spit it out, but no, my jaws are locked. Am I human yet? Or am I still a cat? Or something in between?

The fogginess increases. Please, take me with you. Let me pass out. Let me escape this world.

"What is she saying?"

Am I talking? No, I don't think so.

"She's talking in cat."

No, I'm not.

"It's going to be okay, Kat. I'm here."

His voice is clear, breaking through the fog. Ryker. I cling to his words, holding on as tight as possible. I need him to stay. He's the only one who understands me.

"I'll stay."

Did I say that out loud?

"Yes, you did."

No, I can't have. I can feel my jaws locked together. There's blood in my mouth. I can't talk. I'm trying to but it's not working.

"Kat, you're speaking. A lot. Trust me, you're talking. Yes, there's blood, but your mouth is definitely opening and closing."

But it doesn't feel that way. Does that mean I can't trust anything that I think I feel? Is my body betraying me?

I whimper. Worst. Day. Ever.

"It will be alright," he repeats. "I think your shift is almost over. Hopefully, the bleeding will stop once it's done."

Bleeding?

"Eh, yes, your entire body is covered in blood. It's like you're stuck in between cat and human. Not quite finished. Your skin is still repairing itself."

Urgh, that sounds dreadful. No wonder I'm in agony.

"It looks very painful. One of the humans is looking for painkillers, I think. They're doing their best to help you."

They? I don't understand their voices properly. The only one who feels real is Ryker.

"That must be because you're not quite human yet. But I'm glad you can talk to me. I was so worried."

Worried about me? He should be worried about his son, about the other kittens. It's a waste of time that he's here with me.

"Others are looking for them," Ryker says gently.

"They're keeping me updated. Now that we know that we're looking for another cat shifter, it's just a matter of time until we find her. As soon as my cats find her scent, they'll come and fetch me. And you, if you're feeling better by then. So don't worry. I'll stay."

His words are like medicine. Soothing me, making the pain less. I wonder how he can do that. How he has this sort of power over me.

He chuckles softly. "Maybe it's because I'm a shifter too. Not that I'm fully used to that thought yet. I haven't even told any of the others. If I don't know how to shift, if I'll stay a cat forever, maybe they don't need to know."

He's avoiding the topic.

"No, I'm not. I have thought about it, but I need more time."

How is he responding to all of my thoughts?

"Because you're talking aloud. It seems you have no filter at all. Other cats would take advantage of that."

But he won't. Ryker is a nice cat. Pretty cat. So handsome and sweet and honourable.

He chuckles. "Let me stop you there. Don't say anything you may regret once you're back to normal."

Oh yes. I should be careful. I can't have him know how much I admire him, for how he's helped the other cats, how he's survived without guidance from his parents, how he's managed to get his mane so gorgeous, how-

"Stop, Kat. You're delirious. Are you still in pain?"

I concentrate on my body. It's hard to do, it's like it's not quite my own. Not anymore. There's still pain, but

it's far enough away that it's bearable. But I really want to sleep. Pass out.

"I might be able to help with that. Ever been smothered by a cat?"

I shall add it to my list of weird experiences. My anti-bucket list. I steel myself and hope he can hear my thoughts. Do it. Knock me out.

Something warm and furry touches my face, but because my body is so far away, I don't feel any pain, any discomfort as he slowly suffocates me. Kat, killed by a cat. Oh the irony.

CHAPTER NINE

"Don't you dare wake her. She needs her beauty sleep. Quite literally. Have you seen her skin?"

Meow. Meow.

"Look, you overgrown fur ball. You almost killed her last night. The least you could do is let her sleep."

Meow.

I groan and sit up, looking around the room. I'm not in my hammock, but on the floor, supported by cushions and a blanket. Pity, I love my hammock. It's my favourite part of the day, swinging gently from side to side, pretending I'm outdoors. Unless I did some killing, then that was my favourite part of the day.

"Now you've done it, you've woken her up."

Beth is sitting by the trap door, her legs dangling parallel to the ladder. Ryker is next to her, still meowing. Even though I'm not shifted, it's easy to hear the urgency in his voice. He traipses over to me, rubbing his head against my thigh. I don't remember much of what happened. Lots of pain. My shift going wrong.

"What happened?" I ask Bethany. Urgh, my voice is all hoarse and weak. I need a drink. Milk and honey, or maybe just milk. A whole bowl full. No, glass. Humans drink from glasses.

She grimaces. "You turned into a bloody mess. I'm used to a lot but even I thought it was disgusting. Please don't do it again."

"Do what again?"

Not sure I want to hear, but I hate not having all the information.

"Your fur disappeared but your skin disappeared with it. You were a mass of bloody flesh. That's what happened. As I said, disgusting." She shudders visibly. "And you were meowing a lot. This cat here meowed back, and at some point, he jumped on your face and smothered you. We tried to stop him, but he fought pretty bravely."

She points at scratches on her arms.

I give Ryker a sharp look. "No scratching my friends. They're off limits."

He gives me a scorching glare and I sigh. "Okay, you did good. I dimly remember asking you to do it."

"You asked him to kill you?" Beth asks incredulously.

"Not kill me. Just make me unconscious so I didn't have to feel all that pain."

Her gaze softens. "I'm glad you're still with us. I wasn't all that sure last night. Never seen anything like it, and neither had Lennox."

I perk up. "Lennox was here?"

Ryker growls a little, but I ignore him. This isn't the time for the animosity between cats and wolves.

"Yeah, he left a couple of hours ago when your skin was mostly grown back. He said he'd be back soon, that there was something he needed to do."

Or maybe he's simply avoiding me. I'd do the same.

I turn back to Ryker. "Any news on Pumpkin and the others?"

He shakes his furry head, somehow managing to make it look extremely majestic. Definitely lion's blood somewhere in his family. That mane…

He meows and it's almost like I can understand. His intentions are much clearer than I can usually sense from other cats. For them, it's mostly their basic needs like food, warning of danger, happiness. With him, there's so much more hidden in his meow. It must be because he's a shifter. I've never communicated with other cat shifters - well, I must have as a child, but I can't remember that – so this is a new experience for me.

"What's he saying?" Bethany asks, as if she knows that I can understand.

"They haven't found the kittens yet, but… they found something. And want me to come. Right?"

Ryker nods, relief shining in his bright blue eyes. He meows again.

"You can come along too, Beth. I'm not sure if it's just because you might want to, or because they need you. It's kind of hard to understand."

Beth snickers. "Of course they need me. I'm the best."

I laugh, but stop when my ribs start aching. I seem to be mostly healed, but I should still take it easy. No shifting for several days at the very least. That's going to be torture. Maybe Lennox knows more about what happened. Or maybe he knows other shifters who might. I still don't know who he works for exactly. So many questions I want to ask him, so many stories to hear, but after what happened between us, I'm not sure I'm going to get the chance. Sleeping with him was a mistake. A big one.

Slowly, I get up, realising that I'm naked. I don't really care about Bethany seeing me in the nude, but for some reason, I don't like Ryker seeing me like that. Even though he's a cat. But he's also a male, I remind myself. At some point, he will shift into a human man, once we've figured out how to get him to do that. After the Lennox fiasco, I'm going to stay away from men for a while. No temptations. No nakedness. Definitely no fucking.

"Turn around," I snap, glad when Ryker immediately follows my order. Beth giggles, but doesn't say anything. Good. I feel my strength returning and with it, the desire to kill something. Simply because I'm angry at myself. A good assassination always distracts me from my own failures. Reminds me how good I am at the things that really count.

I quickly get dressed in my favourite black jumpsuit (I have several of them) and pocket as many knives as I can find in the attic. There are more down in the weapons room, but I probably won't get the chance to kill anyone today. If my mother really is the culprit, then I'm not sure I can kill her. I'd have a very violent word with her though. Not just for abandoning me, but also for killing cats and kidnapping babies.

Ryker meows.

"Meet us outside, I'm taking the ladder this time," I tell him and turn to Beth. "You coming?"

She nods. "This is much more interesting than sitting here waiting for Benjamin to wake up."

"Did you analyse the blood yet that was stuck to Haru's claws?"

"Yeah, it's in the machine, but it will take a few more hours till it's done. I've already told Benjamin to compare the results with the police database. He was rather happy when I told him he gets to break into their headquarters again. He was wondering whether they've improved their security since he last did it."

I sigh. "That boy is getting reckless. I'm not going to spend any money on his bail if he gets caught."

Bethany laughs. "I told him exactly that, but he doesn't care. He's good though, he'll manage. You've trained him well."

"There wasn't much training to do. He'd learned most of it himself. I only helped him refine his technique and become a little more soft-footed. Anyway, if that's taken care of, let's go."

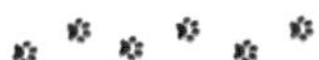

RYKER DOESN'T LEAD US BACK TO THE CHOCOLATE factory, but in the opposite direction. We're slow since I'm not quite strong enough to run, and because I'm munching a sandwich while we're walking. I was starving, since my body apparently used up all my reserves trying to heal itself. I could eat a dozen mice or so. I groan when I realise what I just thought. My mind is still in cat mode. I hope this isn't a permanent thing.

Bethany is whistling cheerily. I'd love to shut her up, but I don't want to spend any energy on arguing with her.

It takes us almost half an hour to reach our destination; a row of nondescript terrace houses. Boring. They all look the same. No personality, no character. The only thing that varies is the state of their front gardens. There's only one that's perfectly kept with grass that looks perfectly even, the rest are everything from overgrown by weeds to covered in rubbish. I wouldn't want to live here.

"What are we doing here?" Beth asks. "This doesn't look like a cat kidnapper would live here."

Ryker meows, but there are too many nuances in his message.

"Sorry, I don't understand. Something about a sign?"

Ryker shakes his head and meows again. This time, there's frustration in the sound, annoyance that I don't get what he's trying to tell me.

"A message?"

He growls in irritation.

"If you're annoyed at me not understanding, maybe you should shift and tell me properly," I snap at him. And regret it instantly.

His eyes widen, the hurt obvious in their blue depths.

I don't say sorry though. It's a word that's not in my vocabulary.

Without another meow, he leads us to a house in the centre of the row. If anyone's looking out of their windows, they must think it's two women taking their cat for a walk, not the other way round. But from the way this neighbourhood looks, I bet everyone is in an office, staring at boring paperwork all day round. How mundane.

There's a narrow gap between two houses, just wide enough for people to drag their bins from the garden to the curb, where rubbish carts come to collect it every couple of days. The garden behind the house is overgrown and doesn't look like anyone's set foot in it for a while. There's a smell in the air though… cats.

Ryker leads us to a large but old shed at the back of the garden. Some of the planks are loose and I bet the roof is leaky.

"Why are we here?" I ask before remembering that I likely won't get a reply I can understand. This is frustrating.

He scratches the shed door and I open it for him. The inside is dark but my eyes adjust quickly. Behind garden equipment and spiderwebs is a pile of dirty outdoor cushions, the ones you use on deck chairs. On top of it is a skinny girl, just as covered in dust as the rest of the shed. Reddish hair shines underneath the dirt, the colour barely visible. She can't be older than five or six, and is staring at us with wide eyes. She doesn't seem scared though, just surprised.

"I did not expect *that*," Beth mutters from behind me.

"Ryker, what's going on?" I ask quietly, not wanting to scare the girl. She's not giving off the scent of someone who's frightened, but until I know what's happening here, I don't want her to run away because she's scared. There has to be a reason why Ryker led us to this shed.

Ryker puts his paw on his nose and pats it.

"You want me to… sniff her?"

He nods.

I step closer to the girl, smiling at her in what I hope looks friendly and unthreatening. I don't think I've got any better in pretending to be nice, but maybe working with children in the Kindler case has made me slightly more approachable. Not that I want to be sociable, but sometimes, giving the appearance of a charming person can come in handy.

She doesn't move, doesn't flinch, just looks at me. I concentrate on my cat senses. They're harder to access; must be a result of my failed shift last night.

Her scent surprises me. No, wrong word. It shocks me. I sniff again, and again, breathing in her scent until I can't concentrate on anything else.

Ryker meows when he realises that I got what he's been trying to tell me.

"What's wrong?" Beth asks when I slowly step back, away from the girl.

I ignore her and lock eyes with the child. "Who are you?"

She doesn't reply.

"What's your name?"

Still no answer.

"Kat, what's going on?" Beth demands.

I clench my fists, unsure how to deal with this.

"She's a shifter," I mutter after a moment's silence. "And I think she's my mother's daughter."

CHAPTER TEN

I need air. I step out of the shed, maintaining composure until I've walked back to the street, out of sight. I'm unsure of how to react. What do you do when you find out that you might have a sister? Scream? Run? Cry? Laugh hysterically? I think I'm closest to the last one, but now that I'm away from the others, I no longer feel like I want to explode. What I want is time travel. Returning to how everything was a couple of weeks ago, before Mr Kindler, before it all went to pieces. Why couldn't things have stayed simple. I had such a lovely life. Now all I have is chaos.

A new scent hits my nose, one that I really don't need just now.

"Go away," I tell Lennox before he even reaches me.

He doesn't listen. He walks to my side and stands there, not quite touching me but close enough that either of us could reach out.

"It was me who found her," he says quietly. "I thought I was tracking the other scent. Your mother's."

"That's not proven yet," I interrupt him brusquely. "It could be someone similar to me. Maybe a distant relative."

"You don't believe that."

I grimace. "No, I don't. But it's a nice delusion that I'd like to hold on to."

Lennox sighs. "Trust me, I totally understand. If one of my parents was to turn up, I don't know what I'd do. Kill them, most likely. And to find out that you have a sister, well, it's overwhelming."

"That's an understatement. I've never, ever thought that I might have siblings. I thought my mother was dead, so there wouldn't have been the possibility. But now she's not dead and I have a sibling and I have no idea what to believe anymore." I look at him, annoyed by the sympathy in his expression. He's not supposed to pity me. I'm the only one who's allowed that. Self-pity is a skill.

"What would you do in my shoes?" I challenge him.

"I haven't got the faintest. I'd probably run and hide under the bridge in the hope that it all goes away."

My anger disappears. We're so similar. I always thought of him as a brother, back at the Pack. Now, he's changed roles, become more than a brother, but already I miss that platonic relationship we had. I'll never be able to look at him again as the boy he once was. I've explored his body from top to bottom, felt him inside me, and turned our relationship upside down into something I can't quite define yet. Not sure if he can, either. We're stumbling in the dark, neither of us experienced enough in relationships to figure it out. For now, avoiding him seems like the best course of action.

"I wasn't sure at first, but Ryker seemed to think the same thing," he says quietly, bringing us back to the topic I don't want to think about. "Her scent is very similar to yours, and now that we know about your mother, figured out what her scent is like, there's little doubt about who she is. Even if we didn't have her scent, she looks like you did at her age. The same hair, the same eyes. You were just as skinny."

His eyes roam my body, his gaze heatens. Is he thinking of what I look like beneath my leather jumpsuit? Is he remembering the way he touched me? For a moment, I let that memory linger in my mind. It's better than facing the fact that I have a half-sister who's in a random shed around the corner. How did she even end up there? Does she live here? Did my mother abandon her too?

"How did I never notice?" I mutter. "If she lives in this town, I must have come across her scent. I've been in this neighbourhood many times before. I know every street, every roof in town. How could I have missed it?"

"You didn't recognise the scent at the chocolate factory either," he says reassuringly. "It's similar to yours, so you probably filed it away as one of your own old traces. You had no reason to think that your mother was alive, nor that there's a sibling of yours living here. I mean, this is mind-blowing. Have you spoken to her yet?"

I shake my head. "I needed a moment alone," I admit, grimacing at my own admission of weakness. I'm becoming a person I never wanted to be. Emotional, dependent on other people, weak. I'm even developing a conscience. This is bad.

"Want me to come with you?" His eyes meet mine. There are so many emotions in his gaze, so many unspoken words. I don't think I can handle them just now.

"No, I need to do this on my own. But stay close, the cats might need you again since we still haven't found my mother."

I know he's thinking that my sister might lead us to her. And yes, I'm already making plans for how I might be able to use the girl as bait. She may be my sister by blood, but I don't know her. I don't owe her anything. I won't harm her, I'd never harm a child, but just because we have the same mother doesn't mean that I'm going to be her loving big sister.

I take a deep breath and make my way back to the shed. Lennox stays behind, but I can feel his gaze boring into my back. I'm almost relieved when I round a corner and I'm out of his line of vision.

Ryker is waiting for me in front of the shed, his body tense. I ignore him and go inside, where Bethany is sitting next to the girl. Neither of them is talking, but there doesn't seem to be any animosity between them. Silently, I take in the child's appearance. Lennox is right, she does look a lot like me. Not just because our hair is the same fiery colour, but the way the tip of her nose looks like someone pressed a finger against it, the straight line of her eyebrows, the shade of her eyes. She's like a tiny version of me. Just as skinny as I was at her age too. Back at the Pack, the oldest and strongest got to eat first, which meant there rarely was enough left over for us younger kids. It's how we learned to be tough, to fight for our right to survive. I scan her thin figure. No muscles are clinging to her arms, no steel in the way she holds herself. She's not a fighter, she's just not had enough food.

Her eyes meet mine, but she doesn't say anything. I'm beginning to wonder if she's mute. Wouldn't a normal child be asking questions? Find out why strangers are coming in her shed, looking at her strangely. How very weird.

"Who are you?" I ask, barely able to hide the bite in my voice. I don't want to scare her, but I'm not comfortable in this situation at all. I almost wish that she'd run away so that I don't have to deal with her.

She doesn't reply. Figures.

I sigh and crouch down until I'm level with her. "I'm Kat. What's your name?"

She doesn't even blink.

"Kat, there's something you need to see," Beth says quietly. She puts a hand on the girl's shoulder and gently lifts her scarf.

"Fuck." I stare at the metal wrapped around my sister's throat. A collar. It's thinner than the one I used to wear, easier to hide underneath clothing, but a collar nonetheless.

I'm ready to kill someone.

"Lennox!" I shout and he appears in the door of the shed only seconds later. He takes in the scene and his expression turns grave.

"Do you have the key to open it?" I ask him, avoiding his eyes. "Do you know how to do it?"

He shakes his head. "I don't, I'm so sorry. I know who might have one though, let me see if I can find him."

I give him a grateful, tight smile and he turns and runs off. Hopefully, he'll be able to find a key. If he doesn't, I might be able to go to Mystery Man's daughter and see if she has his belongings still. He opened my collar, so he must have had a key in his possession.

The girl isn't reacting at all to the fact that we're all staring at her and that Beth is still holding up her scarf. It's as if she's not quite aware of her surroundings. I don't think it's the collar's doing, although maybe this one is different from the one I had. Mine was copper, while this one is a gleaming silver colour. Back at the Pack, there were rumours that there was a new collar they had developed, one that would give them complete control over us, not just over our abilities. I never believed them though. If they'd managed to invent something like that, they would have already been using it.

Now, I doubt myself. I should have believed in their ability to devise even more evil things than the way they'd enslaved us all. We still had minds of our own - tamed, but not completely under their control. If this girl is the result of what they've come up with... I'm going to have to do something about it. This is wrong on so many levels. Lennox has been talking to me about going against the Pack, and so has Lily, but I refused to listen to them. I've tried to stay away from the Pack for so long that actually turning direction and confronting them goes against all I've worked towards. I've wanted to stay in the shadows without drawing attention, focusing on my business, on my life. Doing what I want to do for the first time ever. I've done that for over half a year now. I guess I should have known that it couldn't last forever.

The Pack always catches up with you, even if it's not in the way you expected.

I reach out and run two fingers over the silver collar. It's cold to the touch; again, different from how my own collar used to feel like. It must be uncomfortable, but the girl doesn't react. I grit my teeth and pinch her shoulder. She doesn't even cry out. She just looks at me, the blankness in her eyes obvious now. They may be the same colour as mine, but there is no life in them. She's trapped inside, her mind held hostage by the collar.

I try something else. "Stand up."

Immediately, she does as I say. She sways a little on her thin legs, but I know she won't even notice.

"Those bastards," Bethany whispers. "What have they done to her?"

"Tell me your name," I say firmly, locking eyes with the girl. Before, I asked a question, now, it's a command.

She doesn't respond though. That must mean that either she can't, or she's been forbidden to talk at all.

"Do you live here?" I ask. "Nod if it's a yes."

She shakes her head.

"Then why are you-" I groan when I realise that it won't work that way. Only using yes and no questions will make this take forever. I have no desire to stay here, especially when we don't know why the girl was here in the first place. Are Pack members going to come for her soon? As much as I would love to get my hands on some Pack minions, killing them all very slowly and painfully, I know it's not a good move. We need to prepare and make a plan. Besides, anyone sent here by the Pack would be collared themselves. The people in charge, the ones who don't wear collars, rarely leave their headquarters. They let others do the dirty work, while they enjoy the fruits of their slaves' labour.

"Come with me," I order not unkindly and leave the shed. She stumbles after me and I realise that she's barefoot. Her clothes are torn in places, but they're not bad quality. Her feet, however, are dirty and covered in bruises. Poor thing.

If I could, I'd carry her, but I still feel my own fatigue wearing me down. My body is still healing itself.

Luckily, Gryphon is waiting outside.

"Can you carry her? She looks too frail to make it all the way back to our house."

He nods and gently lifts her in his arms, cradling her against his chest. She doesn't lean against him, doesn't give in to the comfort he tries to give her, but stays stiff and unyielding. Like she doesn't feel it at all.

Again, I want to kill someone. Smash something. Hurt people.

Even if she wasn't my sister, I'd want to avenge what they did to this girl. But since she's my sister... I'm coming for them.

CHAPTER ELEVEN

It takes us longer to get back to the house than I would have liked. It's mostly because I'm slow. Gryphon could probably run all the way even though he's carrying the little girl, but I feel more and more like I'm about to faint. I'm starting to believe that I'm getting ill. That the whole shifting-gone-wrong episode wasn't just because I'd shifted too often. Maybe there's some kind of cat shifter bug. Who knows, it's not like my mother stayed around to teach me.

Yes, I'm bitter. Especially when I look at my little sister. She's half asleep in Gryphon's arms and I almost envy her. She still doesn't look like she has any clue about her surroundings, but she does look more human now that she's so sleepy. I hope the collar will allow her to rest.

By the time we get home, I can barely stand. I don't let any of the others notice that, obviously, but putting up a strong façade uses up even more of my limited energy.

"Let's take her to the living room," I tell Gryphon and let him walk ahead, followed by Ryker and two other, smaller cats. Bethany is by my side, quiet and lost in thought.

I lean against the doorframe and watch as he carefully lays her on one of the sofas, supporting her little head. He's so gentle with the little girl. I'm surprised to see this side of him. It makes him even more intriguing. He's a mystery that I still need to solve. Hell, I don't even know what he is. Usually, I wouldn't let someone close to me who I don't know anything about, but he's proved that he's trustworthy. In the way any assassin can be trusted. Benjamin runs down the stairs, trips and lands on all fours in front of my feet. I sigh. And this is supposed to be my master thief? The boy who can get into any building unnoticed, even the heavily guarded police headquarters? Yeah, sure.

He grins at me and jumps to his feet.

"You look tired," he observes. Oh, how I'm tempted to slap him. But good employers don't hit their staff. I'm not going to win Employer of the Year anytime soon, but I don't want any of them to leave. They're too invaluable – even Benjamin.

"At least you're no longer covered in blood. How are you feeling?"

I'm taken aback by that question. People don't usually ask me that. My glare shuts them up before they ever get the idea of asking me such a mundane, unnecessary question.

I nod towards the girl instead. "Meet my sister."

His eyes widen. "Are you serious?"

I grimace. "As serious as I can be. Half-sister. Same mother. Can you get her some food? For all of us, actually. Lots and lots of food."

He looks as if he'd rather go over to the sofa and investigate, but luckily, he decides to follow my order. I slowly walk to one of the armchairs, pretending to be slow for a good reason, not because I'm about to keel over. Still, when I hit the fluffy cushions, I can't help but sigh in relief.

Gryphon is examining the girl, expertly checking her vitals. He lifts her shirt a little, exposing ribs that protrude more than they should. She's not just thin, she's extremely malnourished. It was hidden underneath her clothes before, but I'm starting to get worried about her. And angry at whoever neglected her.

She's fast asleep now. Lucky her.

"Once she wakes up, we need to get some food in her," Gryphon says. Stating the obvious. Even I would have known that, and I'm much better with killing than with healing.

Benjamin returns and hands me a large mug of tea. Heaven in a cup. I start drinking immediately, burning my gums, but I don't care. Maybe this will give me some of the energy I sorely lack. When he gives me a plate full of ham sandwiches, I fall in love with him.

"You're my hero," I mutter, my mouth already full of food.

"I thought I was your hero," Gryphon quips. He's sat down at the end of the sofa the little girl is lying on and is slowly sipping some tea. He's all in black, as always, but the way he holds his cup makes him look like an aristocrat rather than a thug. I wonder what kind of upbringing he had. Something posh? Is he some kind of wealthy rebel, someone who does his because he enjoys it rather than because he has to.

Not that I don't enjoy it, but I never had much of a choice. I was trained to be a killer. My education wasn't history, politics, grammar. We were taught to read and write, but that was about it. Our other lessons were about how the human body worked, how it could be hurt, how poisons would impact organs and flesh. Lockpicking rather than maths. Breaking and entering instead of physics.

"How did you find us? How did you know that we might need you?" I ask instead of all the other questions I need answers to. They can wait, for now.

Gryphon points at the little cat lying at his feet. She looks like a hairball another cat has thrown up. More fluff than cat. Her fur would probably be white if she wasn't covered in dirt. For all my love of cats, I couldn't call her pretty. Unique, maybe. That's as far as I can go.

"This little furball came to find me. I assume Ryker sent her?"

The larger cat nods in confirmation. Benjamin has given him a bowl of water and I bet there will be some treats coming soon. That boy has fallen in love with the cats, and has become an expert at spoiling them. I bet he knows every single cat's favourite treat.

"I didn't have any other plans, so I followed her. But I think you have some explaining to do. Who is she? Why are you saying she's your sister? I mean, the similarity is obvious, but it seems like you didn't know about her? How's that even possible?"

I groan. "Too many questions. She's my mother's daughter, because yes, my mother is alive even though I thought she was dead. No idea who her father is. Her scent is similar to mine, which is why the cats thought they were tracking my mother, rather than her. She's not spoken a single word, so we have no idea what's happened to her or where she's come from. Basically, we don't know anything. Lennox is trying to find a key to open her collar, maybe that will enable her to speak to us. Until then-"

A wave of dizziness overcomes me and I close my eyes for a second.

"Are you alright?"

His voice contains a surprising amount of concern.

I force my eyes open to look at him. "I'm fine. Just a bit tired."

"She lost a lot of blood," Bethany blurts. I could kill her. "Kat, you should lie down and get some rest. You look like you're about to faint."

Is it that obvious?

"I'm fine. Pumpkin and the other kittens are still missing. This has cost us valuable time."

Ryker gets up and rubs against my legs. I meet his bright blue eyes, as deep as the sea. I've never seen the ocean, but I imagine it to be like Ryker's eyes, full of swirling shades of blue. Mysterious. Beautiful.

He meows, conveying a strange mixture of worry and reassurance.

"Yes, I know your cats are still out there looking for

my mother's scent, but I might be able to find her faster if I was able to shift. She's my mother, she's my responsibility."

He meows again, more forcefully this time.

"Don't worry, I'm not stupid enough to shift anytime soon. I didn't enjoy being suffocated by you."

Gryphon lifts a questioning eyebrow and I realise that it must have sounded strange without context. I don't waste energy on explaining it though. My thoughts are turning sluggish. I really need to get some sleep, but no, I can't afford to waste any more time. Who knows what's happening to Pumpkin just now. I hadn't realised how attached I'd become to the little kitten, but now that he's gone, I want to do anything I can to get him back.

"We should go and…"

Darkness overwhelms me before I can even finish my sentence.

I DON'T KNOW HOW LONG I SLEEP. IT'S NOT ENOUGH though. When I wake up, I'm still tired. Not quite as exhausted, but still not as awake as I'd like to be. I'm still in the armchair in the living room. Someone's put a blanket over my legs. Seriously? Do they think I'm an old woman who needs a blanket? I need to teach them that I'm not weak, not in the slightest. Things are getting out of control and I can't afford to lose my reputation.

The little girl is still asleep, but there are crumbs on

her shirt now. She must have eaten something while I slept. Good.

Everyone else has left, so I let myself yawn and stretch for a while, before getting up from the armchair. I half expect the world to sway again, but besides a slight weakness in my knees, I'm feeling much better.

I listen to the sounds of the house. Someone's downstairs in the lab, rummaging in cupboards. I concentrate on the scent. Bethany. I can't sense Benjamin anywhere, but Gryphon is in the kitchen. What is he still doing here? His scent is mixed with that of salty broth. Is he making soup? Now that's something I have to see.

Slowly, I walk to the kitchen. I might be able to walk faster now, but I want to conserve my energy as much as possible. This feels like a moment of peace before the storm. I better enjoy it while it lasts.

"You're up," Gryphon says without turning around.

"Stating the obvious. What are you doing?"

"Making soup. The girl had trouble eating solid food, so I thought this might be better for her." He continues stirring the broth without looking at me. My mouth is starting to water. It smells delicious.

I walk over to his side and take a spoon from a drawer. "I need to test it for poison," I tell him and dip my spoon into the soup.

He chuckles. "Obviously."

The soup doesn't just smell delicious, it also tastes amazing. "What did you put in there?" I ask. "Some kind of miracle spices?"

Gryphon laughs. "Exactly. Secret ingredients like

carrots, parsley and parsnips. Which are so secret that they're hidden in plain sight, without actually being hidden."

He points at the carrot peels to his left. Yeah, right. As if. Carrots don't taste this good. At least not when I try to cook them. And parsnips, they're just white ugly carrots. Definitely not as divine tasting as whatever he's put in his soup.

"Give it another ten minutes to stew, then you'll get a whole bowl full," he promises. "The others told me what happened to you. The fluids will be good for you. Losing that amount of blood isn't to be taken lightly, even as a shifter."

I scoff. "So you're a doctor now?"

"In a way."

"Wait, you're a doctor?"

"I never finished my exams, but I studied long enough to know the basics. But even a blind person could see that you're not at your full strength just now. You need to rest."

"I don't have time to rest. Besides, you don't look like a doctor."

He turns to me and frowns. "Because of my scars?"

"I don't care about your scars. Because you wear tight black clothes that hide more weapons than even I carry, because you move like a predator about to pounce at his prey, because your eyes show how many people you've killed. Doctors save lives, they don't take them."

He smiles sadly. "Sometimes, you have to take a life to save another. Just because I kill bad people doesn't mean that I don't care about the wellbeing of the good."

"The world isn't black and white. You can't divide people into good and bad."

"Isn't that what you do when you kill?"

I shake my head. "I don't distinguish. If I get paid, I do the job. I don't care whether the person I terminate has done amazing things for society or killed a dozen people. Well, I might be a little more violent if it's the latter, but I still kill for money. That's what I am. An assassin. Not a vigilante."

His frown deepens. "I don't believe that."

"Then don't." I laugh harshly. "People keep thinking that I'm a good person because I'm a woman, because I'm young, because I don't look like they imagine a villain to look. But inside, I'm cold. I'm a weapon, Gryphon, and just because I occasionally seem to show some semblance of humanity doesn't mean that it's real."

"If you really believe that, you're lying to yourself. I've seen you save those kids. I've seen how you care for the cats that frequent this house. And earlier, when you looked at the little girl, there was something beautiful in your eyes."

"And what was that?"

"Love."

I laugh, but there's no humour in the sound. "I don't love. Just ask Lennox."

The last sentence slips out before I can stop myself.

He smiles at me, not reacting to that statement. "Ever thought about therapy?"

I gape at him. "Are you for real? Did whoever claw your face mess with your brain?"

"Now you're getting defensive. Is that what you do? Push people away as soon as they get close?"

"You're not close. You're nowhere near close. And you'll never be."

I storm out of the kitchen. I lied. He got close. Not to me, but to the truth.

I hate him for it.

CHAPTER TWELVE

"Take my blood."

"Huh?" Bethany looks at me in confusion.

"Check it for infections. I should be back to normal by now. I'm a shifter, I heal fast. I think there might be something wrong with me. Maybe some kind of virus."

"You do know that I have no idea about what kind of bugs cats might get?"

I sigh. "Just check for increased white blood cell count. That should at least give us an idea on whether there's an infection."

She nods and gets her equipment. She's somehow turned into our lab person, even though that's not what she excels at. Lily used to spend a lot more time down here, experimenting with poisons, but then she started taking on more cases that involved her using her skills of seduction, so Bethany took over a lot of Lily's tasks. She's good at it though. She immediately finds my vein and starts taking my blood until she's got two vials filled.

"If you want, I can compare it to the blood I took

from the cat's claws," Beth says quietly. "I know we all think that it's that of your mother, but shall I make sure it really is?"

"Do it."

"Alright. It won't take long. I'll let you know as soon as I have a result. Until then, you could spend time with sexy Gryphon?"

I snort. "Did you just call him sexy?"

Bethany shrugs and wiggles her eyebrows. "Have you looked at him? Those scars only make him look even more like a hot bad boy. Unless you and Lennox are exclusive?"

"Okay, I'm leaving now. I won't be having girly conversations."

She laughs. "Wait, you've still got the cannula stuck in your arm."

Oh. So I have. I let her remove it, but ignore the band aid she tries to hand me. I don't need something as human as that. The wound will seal itself in a couple of seconds.

"You know where I am, if you ever want a girls talk," Beth says with a giggle. "I'd love to find out more about your love life."

"I don't have a love life," I growl. "Why the fuck is everyone using the L-word today?"

"Everyone? Did Gryphon confess his undying love for you?"

"His undying- for fuck's sake. Stop it."

I storm out of the room, slamming the door shut for dramatic effect. Why is everyone acting weird today? Is it a full moon yet? Some kind of hormone fluctuation?

Since all the adults in this house are being strange, I decide to check on the girl again.

She's awake, but staring blankly at the ceiling, not reacting to me entering the room at all. Not even her heartbeat increases. It's like all her senses are turned off. Standby mode.

I kneel in front of the sofa and simply watch her for a bit. The longer I look at her, the more striking the similarities between us become. I have no idea if I take after my mother or my father, since I can't remember what either of them looked like, but now that I see my sister, it must be my mother who gave us our looks. I wonder who the girl's father is. Is he still alive? Is my mother in love with him? Married to him? In effect, that would make him my stepfather. No thanks. I don't need a family. Yesterday morning, I was all on my own. Now I have a sister and a mother that's turned out to be alive. Life is moving a little too fast for me.

"Sit up," I command, and the girl does it immediately. Her back is straight as a board and while she looks in my direction, she doesn't look *at* me. Her eyes are blank.

"Can you write?" I ask, hopeful that this might be a solution to her not being able to speak.

She shakes her head. There goes that idea.

"Alright, I'm going to ask you some yes and no questions and I want you to answer them truthfully. Do you understand?"

She nods.

I feel bad for how harsh I'm being, how I'm ordering

her around, but this seems to be the only way to get her to react.

"Are you part of the Pack?"

She nods and my heart sinks. I mean, the collar made it kind of obvious, but because it looked different than my own one had, I still had a flicker of hope that she might have been under the control of someone else. Like my mother. Just one person, easy to deal with. Not the entire Pack.

"Will they be searching for you?"

She shrugs. At least it's not an outright yes.

"Have they hurt you?"

There's the tiniest of pauses before she nods. A cold shiver runs down my back. She's not even able to cry. Not able to ask for help. She's forced to accept her plight.

I need to kill something, soon. The anger in me is spreading and I know that if I don't get it under control, my panther will want to take over. Which would probably kill me, and I'm far too selfish to let it do that.

"Do you know who she is?" Bethany steps into the room, asking the question without giving me any explanation. "Do you know who the woman in front of you is?"

The girl nods.

"That's what I thought. Kat, we need to talk. Now."

I stare at her in confusion, but then follow her out of the room and into the hallway.

"Ben!" Bethany shouts. "Come down and watch over the girl for a bit!" She turns to me and lowers her voice. "We can't leave her alone in there. I don't know why she's here, but I doubt it's because she wants a family reunion."

"We brought her here," I protest. "She had no choice in the matter."

"Didn't she? When we found her, did she try to run? Did she seem like she didn't want to go with us, strangers?"

"No, but she's wearing a collar. She doesn't have the capacity to express her own opinion. She probably doesn't even know where she is."

"I wish I could believe that," Bethany mutters and slowly walks into the dining room. I follow her, not quite sure what she's on about. I wait while she pours us two cups of tea. It's only lukewarm, but I think she needs this moment to collect her thoughts, to decide how to break her news to me.

I take one sip of tea and then decide that I don't want any more of it. I hate cold tea.

"While you were asleep, I took a blood sample from her," Bethany starts, her voice quiet. "Not because I wanted to know whether she really was your sister, but because I wanted to do a health check on it, see what kind of nutrients she's missing the most so that we could help her get back to full strength quickly. Well, when you came down and gave me some of your own blood, I thought I'd compare it, just for... for fun, I guess. Maybe it was intuition, I don't know."

"What did you find?" I interrupt her. "What's so special about her blood?"

Bethany takes a deep breath. "It's like yours."

"Of course it's like mine, we have the same mother."

"No, you don't get it. It's *exactly* like yours. Your DNA is identical. Not just similar like it should be for siblings. Identical. Do you understand what that means? She's not your sister, Kat. She's your clone."

I DRINK THAT COLD TEA AFTER ALL. AND THEN BETHANY makes us a new pot of tea. I feel more like downing an entire bottle of whisky, but I need my mind clear to think.

At some point, Bethany leaves and returns with Gryphon. I can sense Benjamin in the living room together with the girl. The child who I thought was my sister. Even though I only met her earlier today, I feel it almost as a loss. I no longer have a sister. It was just an illusion. Instead, she's a construct, a copy of me, created for reasons that I haven't figured out yet.

"Bethany," I say when a rogue thought enters my mind. "Did you compare my mother's blood with mine yet?"

She shakes her head. "The girl's sample was already in the machine, so I did hers first. We analysed you mother's DNA, but haven't matched it with your own yet."

"Then do it now. Compare the blood sample we got from the crime scene with that of the girl and my own."

Gryphon sucks in a sharp breath. "You think we got it wrong?"

I nod grimly. "I think we have."

"What are you saying?" Bethany asks with a frown. "I'm not getting it."

"She thinks that her mother may never have been there at all," Gryphon explains. I gladly let him do the talking. My mind is far too chaotic right now to form coherent sentences. "We assumed it was her mother because it was the scent of a jaguar shifter and very similar to that of Kat. She thought she remembered it as that of her mother. But what if we all got it wrong? What if it was the clone who killed the cats?"

Bethany gasps. "I don't believe that. I mean, look at her. She's tiny, she's vulnerable, she's young. She wouldn't be able to kill two grown cats, let alone kidnap six kittens."

"She's a shifter," I say quietly. "She may look like a little girl, but she is much stronger than you think. At her age, the Pack taught me to kill. If she's been with them since birth, who knows how well they've trained her already."

"But you said you smelled your mother's scent," Bethany insists.

"I thought that it was hers. Now, I'm not so sure. The girl doesn't have exactly the same scent as I do, but it's very similar. It's been a long time since I last saw my mother. My memory could have deceived me. It was the most logical conclusion at the time, but now that we know that she's my... that she's not really my sister, it's all starting to make sense."

"Let's say it was her," Gryphon says, running his hands over his stubbly beard. "Then why would she kidnap kittens? What's the point? What would the Pack want with a bunch of baby cats?"

I shrug. "Your guess is as good as mine. The Pack has many layers, who knows what they're planning. I was their only cat shifter and some of their researchers were fascinated with me. Luckily, I was one of the best at my job, so they didn't get to prod and examine me as much as they wanted to."

"Maybe that's why they created a clone. To have the time and opportunity to study another cat shifter. They've seen you in action, they know what you can do, but they haven't been able to tame you. Otherwise, we wouldn't all be in this room just now."

I grimace. "They certainly tried to tame me, but you're right, they never controlled me like they did the others. I think some of them preferred that, because I was able to change strategy if something went wrong during a job. The others would just follow the commands of their leaders, unable or unwilling to use their own brains."

"So now they've created a miniature you," he says thoughtfully. "They've got her under complete control. Maybe that collar was custom made for her, based on whatever observations they did on you. But if they liked you because you were able to think for yourself, then why completely subdue her?"

"That's why I have Benjamin watching her," Bethany says quickly. "I don't think that she's as harmless as she seems. She might have orders to wait and act at the perfect moment. Or maybe she was sent to infiltrate us. The Pack knows about us, knows about you, Kat. Harming some local cats would have been the perfect way to draw you out."

I scoff. "If they wanted me to face them, they could have sent me a message. Half the criminals in this town have my business card by now."

"That's exactly what they don't want," Gryphon mutters. "They didn't want you to know. They probably hoped that you'd jump to the most plausible conclusion: that the girl is your sister, or maybe a cousin. They wouldn't have expected us to immediately figure out that she's a clone."

"I was the one who figured it out," Bethany interjects. "Don't forget that. And be sure to tell Lily when she returns that I'm the queen of the lab now. She can assist me occasionally, if she asks nicely."

I can't suppress an amused snort. "You can let her know yourself. I won't get in between the two of you. Do that cat fight on your own."

"Nice pun," Gryphon says, but he's not smiling. "But what do we do now? The girl has seen where you live. She's seen Lennox, Bethany, Benjamin and me. She can tell them that you don't work alone. She might look like she's a zombie, but I bet she's taking in every detail around her, ready to tell her masters everything."

I swallow hard, trying to get this image he's painting in line with the little girl that carries my genes. She doesn't look like a spy, but he's right, that's exactly the point. Who would suspect a child, one looking so thin and helpless at that. The Pack will have realised during the Kindler case that I seem to have a soft spot for children. Even though it was the Fangs who'd organised the whole thing, the Pack were involved, I'm convinced of that. We may have killed all the Fang contacts we found in town, but I bet there are others lurking in the shadows.

"Lennox is trying to get the key to open her collar. If we manage to remove it, we might be able to have a proper conversation with her, or at least find out if she's just following orders or if they've brainwashed her to really be a threat to us. Right now, we don't have the full picture. For now, we keep an eye on her and don't let her leave the living room. I don't want her to see the rest of the house, if she is indeed sent as a spy."

Gryphon nods. "Let's hope your wolf will find a key. Are there any other ways to open a collar? I know a welder who might be able to cut it open."

"No, that would kill her," I say, remembering the pain every attempt to get the collar off resulted in. "The collar is programmed to torture its wearer unless it's opened with the correct key. Trust me, we tried everything to get rid of them."

Bethany shudders. "Have I ever told you that I'm grateful not to be a shifter? I might not get all fluffy and cute like you do, but at least nobody is trying to enslave me."

"Fluffy? Cute?" I give her a playful growl. "You're talking to a predator, not a pussy cat."

"And that's exactly why I'm worried," Gryphon says, not cracking a smile. "That girl is a predator. She may look cute, but until we know her intentions, we have to treat her like an enemy."

Everything inside of me fights against the idea of

the girl, my clone, being a threat, but I know he's right. His logic is sound.

"Alright, I'm going back in there to see if I can get any more information out of her. She seems to be programmed to follow any command given to her, so I hope all her answers are truthful."

"Unless that's what they want you to think," Gryphon interjects.

Bethany rolls her eyes. "Has anyone ever told you that you're very pessimistic?"

"Cautious," he corrects. "There's a difference. If you'd experienced what I have, you'd be the same."

"Want to expand on that?"

"No." His expression immediately hardens. Damn that man, he wants us to trust him but he doesn't tell us anything about himself. At least we know now that he's got some medical knowledge. That might come in handy.

"Guys!"

We exchange a look, then follow Benjamin's shout into the living room. He's lying on the ground, the girl on his chest, a knife pressed against his throat. Where the fuck did she get a knife from? I'm sure Gryphon would have found it when he examined her. She must have taken it from somewhere in the room while nobody was watching. Damn.

"Let him go," I command, but she doesn't even look at me. So much for her having to follow orders. Not ours, obviously.

Slowly, very slowly, I reach for the bundle of poisoned arrows attached to the inside of my belt. The deadly ones are on the right, but I take one that will only put her to sleep. I have no intentions of killing her. She holds too many answers for that, and besides, I'm starting to accept that I have a soft spot for kids.

"Put down the knife," I say as firmly as I can. Last chance.

She doesn't react. The blade is pressed hard against Benjamin's neck. It would only need a bit more pressure to break his skin. I need to be careful about this. I don't want to lose my thief. There's no way back from a cut throat. A stabbing wound somewhere else, yes, maybe, but not with his aorta cut and his windpipe injured. My sleep darts take about a second to take effect. That would be long enough for her to act, so I need to distract her somehow.

I reach for my panther, ignoring the pain. I'm not going to shift, I'm not suicidal, but I connect with her enough to let out a loud meow. Not a threatening sound, more of a greeting.

The girl whirls around, looking at me in surprise, giving me the opening to throw my dart. It hits her in the neck, just where I intended. Her eyes widen and for a second, I can see the girl behind the collar, frightened and angry. Then the poison starts to act and she collapses on top of Benjamin.

"Thanks," he groans and rolls her off him. "Next time, warn me if I'm guarding a psychopath. I was trying to get her to play with me and suddenly she's holding a knife to my throat. Crazy."

He rubs his neck. There's a tiny cut, but it's negligible.

I pick up the knife, examining it closely. It's one of mine, one of several that are stashed all around the house. I thought they were hidden well, but apparently this girl was able to find one with ease. I get on my knees by her side and search her for weapons. There's another knife down her sleeve, but this one isn't mine.

I show it to the others. "Does this belong to one of you?"

Gryphon's eyes widen and he snatches it from my hand. "She must have taken it while I was carrying her here. Guess that proves that she's been playing us."

"We've been fools," Bethany sighs. "What are we going to do now?"

I look down at the little girl, who seems to be sleeping peacefully. The poison will keep her asleep for at least two hours, unless I give her the antidote. Hopefully, Lennox will return by then. Otherwise, I'll have to drug her again. Having her conscious is too much of a risk.

"Now, we come up with a plan."

CHAPTER THIRTEEN

R yker returns, but Lennox doesn't. I'm going to give him another hour, and if he's not back by then, I'm going to figure out how to contact the daughter of my mysterious benefactor. I somehow doubt that she knows about the key or what it looks like, but it's our only other way to get the collar off the girl. Unless we break into the Pack headquarters and steal one from there. Unlikely. I'm not going anywhere near the Pack until I know what they're after. I have no idea about cloning, but I assume that the girl was born as a baby, not somehow created as a child, which would mean that they started planning this many years ago, while I was still part of the Pack. That makes it even more frightening. There are so many variables that we don't know.

She might be tasked with drawing me out just now, but that's not what she was created for. Did she take those kittens simply to get my attention or is there another reason? What would anyone use kittens for? It's not like cats taste particularly good. They're not like dogs either who often suffer from Stockholm syndrome. No, cats don't forget if they were mistreated. These kittens will never willingly stay with their captors. They will always try to get back home. Especially Pumpkin, who knows his father will be out there, looking for him.

My heart aches when I think of the kitten. He's full of spunk and courage, but he's still only a child.

Ryker gives the tied-up girl a questioning look, rubbing against her thigh.

"She's not as innocent as she looks," I say with a sigh and explain what happened. When I get to the part of us thinking that it might have been the girl who killed Mila and Haru, he hisses and jumps away from her. He looks at me, his eyes full of pain.

"I'm sorry," I mutter. "I know it was easier to think that it was my mother, an adult gone crazy, blinded with grief, whatever. Now we're stuck with a five-year-old child who may have killed cats and kidnapped kittens, who was sent here to spy on me. It's hard to swallow."

He meows questioningly and I think I understand what he's asking.

"Keep your cats looking for her scent. Maybe that will give us some indication on where she's been or what she's done. If we're lucky, she didn't bring the kittens to the Pack headquarters but hid them somewhere."

He nods and runs out of the room; I assume to talk to his family and give them new instructions.

"Wait, Ryker!"

A meow, then he's back.

"Do you have someone following Lennox?"

He nods, giving me a glare that tells me that I'm asking stupid questions, again.

"We need him to hurry up. Have your cats show him that it's urgent. Maybe some scratches and a bite or two."

Bethany chuckles. "Are you asking him to have your boyfriend tortured?"

"He's not my boyfriend," I growl. "And if you insinuate that one more time, I'm going to get every cat in this town to harass you."

She mutters something under her breath, too quiet for even me to hear. I don't think it's a compliment, but I ignore her.

Ryker leaves and this time, I let him. Now it's just the Meow team left. Benjamin, Bethany and me. I kind of miss Lily. She's missing out on a lot. I doubt her succubus festival is as exciting as what's happening here. Probably a lot less deadly, too.

I watch the girl as her chest gently lifts with every breath. She's sleeping peacefully and seems more relaxed than when we got her here. Must be the poison's effect. Once again, I'm struck by how similar she is to me. I wonder what her name is. Did they call her Katriona the second? Did they even give her a proper name or does she have a number?

Even though she threatened to kill Benjamin, I still feel for her. I know what wearing a collar felt like, even though it never controlled me as much as it did everyone else. It dampens your emotions, makes it harder to think. When someone tells you to do something, it feels as if there's no other way but to do it.

Benjamin enters the room, covered in cat hair. "The kittens are fine," he says with a sheepish smile. I hope this is him apologising for shouting at me. When I told him who the girl is, he got a little upset that I brought a kitten thief into our headquarters, a house that is currently home to seven kittens. I mean, he's got a point, but that's irrelevant. It's not like we could have left her all alone in that shed, and we didn't know she was the cat killer until later, anyway.

A sound outside makes me sit up straight, but I relax a little when his scent hits my nose. Lennox. Finally.

I jump off the sofa and go to meet him.

"Did you get the key?" I shout before he's even entered the house.

He steps through the door and triumphantly waves a small object in his hand. Relief floods me. Finally, something good is happening. Now we just need to hope that the key works on this new kind of collar.

LENNOX LOOKS WORRIED AFTER I'VE EXPLAINED WHAT'S happened. "Do you think there are more clones?"

"I've not thought of that," I admit. "There could be, for all I know. Until we know why they made her, we need to assume anything and everything."

"Imagine, a hundred little Kats," he mutters. "Not sure if that's fun or the stuff of nightmares."

"For me, nightmares. I like there being just one of me."

He avoids my eyes. "I know. You like being on your own."

I don't deign him with a reply. At some point, we might have to talk about what happened, but for now, I'm very happy ignoring it. We have more important things to deal with, anyway.

"Shall we wake her up first or do it with her asleep?" he asks, handing me the key. It doesn't look what I imagined at all. No key as such, but a smooth palm-sized stone with strange markings engraved in it. I'm not sure what it's made from, but it doesn't look like any mineral I know of. It's cold to the touch and heavier than it should be.

"Let's do it while she's asleep," I say, remembering how irritating it can be when a collar is removed. When they did it to us as children, they chained us to a chair, making sure that we couldn't move at all. Back when Mystery Man removed my collar, it was only because he somehow knew how to make me focus, that I didn't go crazy.

"Good idea. I went feral for a long time," Lennox mutters, his expression pained. "And we don't know what she's like without a collar."

"Exactly. She could be a trained killing machine without a conscience." I'm not quite believing that though, not after I saw her eyes just before she fell unconscious. There was life in there. Hope.

"How do I do this?" I ask, kneeling by the girl's side. I barely remember how my own collar was removed.

"Hold the key in one hand and try and open the clasp at the back of the collar with your other," Lennox instructs. "I think that's all you need to do. Everyone, get ready, who knows what will happen when the collar gets removed."

Gryphon lazily swirls a knife in his hand, looking seemingly relaxed, but the underlying tension in his body shows that he's ready to attack. Bethany and Benjamin stand behind him. Neither of them are experts at fighting in hand to hand combat - Beth much prefers to do her killing with poisons and Benjamin isn't much of an assassin at all - but the more of us, the better, even if it's just for blocking the door so she can't escape.

Ryker is by my side, so close that his fur touches my legs. If he was human, I'd have pushed him away long ago, but as a cat, he has certain privileges.

"Let's hope this works," I mutter, and reach out to touch the collar. It's cold, colder than the stone that I'm clutching in my other hand. The girl's skin is red and chafed where the collar sits, but I doubt she even feels it in that strange zombie state she's in.

I fumble for the clutch that keeps the collar in place. When I touch it, a jolt of electricity runs through it from the collar right into the hand that's holding the key. The clutch is smaller than the one on my own collar used to be, but even so, it's easy enough to open with one hand.

With a clicking sound, the collar jumps open and slides off the girl's neck. I gently pull it off her, waiting to see how she'll react. She's still sleeping and her arms and legs are tied, but that doesn't mean that something won't happen.

Slowly, I step back, not taking my eyes off her. Her eyes are closed, but her heart rate is increasing. She's waking up.

"Get ready," I say quietly, even though I know that the others are well prepared.

The girl's breathing grows faster, too fast. Suddenly, her eyes rip open, her pupils dark, almost black. She gasps for air, clutches her throat. Is she suffocating?

Without warning, she shifts, faster than I've ever seen anyone shift. One second, she's a girl, next second, she's a black panther. A lot smaller than when I shift, but still at least twice as large as Ryker. He extends his claws, ready for a confrontation.

The ropes lie curled up on the floor, no longer holding her back. She growls, looks around with those dark eyes of hers, but she doesn't attack. The tension is her is evident though, and I doubt it will take much to set her off. She's confused, disoriented, but not aggressive. We need to keep it that way.

Slowly, very slowly, I crouch down, making myself less threatening. I lift my arms, hoping that even as a shifter, she still has a basic understanding of human gestures.

"We're not here to hurt you," I tell her quietly, but determinedly. While I don't want her to think we're a threat, we can't seem like prey either.

Her head whips from side to side as she takes all of us in. I hope Gryphon is no longer playing with his knives, but I don't dare turn around to check.

She seems unsure, as if she can't decide whether we're her enemies or not. I wish I could shift. It would make things so much easier. She's in cat mode just now and I doubt she'll be able to shift back and talk to us properly.

Ryker meows softly and slowly steps forward, his tail touching my leg. In a strange urge to protect him, I almost reach down to keep him back, but I resist that need. He's an adult, he knows what he's doing.

The intention of his meows is so strong that I bet the others can understand him too. He's telling the girl that we're no threat, that we want to help. That we want to keep her safe. He promises her our protection, maybe even our friendship.

She cocks her head to one side. Does she understand what he's saying? I've always been able to understand cats when I'm shifted, but who knows if that's the same for her. She's a clone, it could be different.

Finally, after Ryker repeats it all several times, she relaxes a little. Not enough yet to make me think that she'll be easy to deal with, but enough to slightly ease the tension in my limbs.

To my surprise, Ryker holds out a paw to the girl. She stares at it. I really hope she doesn't think he's offering her to bite him. Or eat his paw. Who knows what she's been raised like.

Slowly, she raises her own paw – much bigger than Ryker's – and nudges his. Like a cat handshake. Strange. I'm not sure what Ryker is trying to achieve with this, but it seems to be working.

She looks at their paws, different in size but similar in looks. His fur isn't quite as black and silky as hers, but it's close enough. I think he's showing her that he's the same. If she's my only clone, that means she's probably never met another cat shifter before.

Ryker meows and this time, she replies. Her voice is soft and high-pitched, but beautiful. Not quite my own, I think, but who knows what my voice sounds like outside my head.

"What are they saying?" Gryphon whispers, not realising that I don't have a clue. I don't respond.

Back and forth they meow, until the little panther bows her head. Wow, I didn't expect her to show respect for Ryker. After all, she's been sent by the Pack. Not exactly my friends.

Ryker steps back until he's rubbing against my legs once again. Now that I know he's a shifter and not just a cute cat, that gesture has more meaning than I would like. He's basically a man with lots of fur and claws. Well, not a man, but a male. Men don't just rub against women unless they want something. Or are in a relationship.

Without warning, the girl shifts from panther back to human. How can she do it that fast? The change is almost instant, without the pain I usually have to suffer through. Maybe I shifted that fast when I was a child, before I was with the Pack? I can't remember, and I wasn't allowed to shift until I was a teenager, and when I did, they immediately put a collar on my panther. From the way she looks at her world with wonder and surprise, I bet this is the first time she's ever been without a collar.

She stares right at me, my own eyes being reflected back at me.

"Hello, Kat."

CHAPTER FOURTEEN

S he knows my name. Not that it should surprise me, but it's kind of creepy to see my younger self say my name.

"Hello. What shall I call you?"

She frowns at me. "Kat, of course. That's my name."

"No, that's my name," I protest. "We can't have the same one."

Her frown deepens in genuine confusion. "Why not?"

"Because..." I don't want to set her off or make her think that we're not on her side, so I need to be careful with what I say. Diplomacy, Kat. It's a virtue. One that I really don't possess. "Because it will get confusing for my friends," I say, quickly making up an excuse. "Two Kats in one room might be too hard for them."

Gryphon chuckles.

"Some of them aren't very bright," I add and his chuckles stop.

"Then we can call you Katriona." She shrugs. "I've never much liked that name."

Okay, she's evil. And so like me. I've always preferred Kat too, not quite happy with the name my parents gave me.

"*Katriona*, I'll make us some tea," Bethany announces with glee. "Kat, would you like tea or maybe some hot chocolate?"

The girl looks confused. "Chocolate melts when it gets hot, why would I want that? It gets sticky."

Bethany gasps theatrically. "You've never had a hot chocolate? I shall make you one, you're going to love it."

She disappears from the room. She's been very friendly to my clone, as if she's forgotten that this child has killed two cats and kidnapped a bunch of kittens. It probably wasn't her choice, but I think we need to be cautious. I don't want to trust her, because I know how deceiving I can be.

"Let's sit down," I suggest and point at the sofa closest to her. "Are you hungry?"

Gryphon fed her some broth earlier, but children at this age can be ravenous, especially after a shift.

She nods, and I turn to the assassin. "Can you get her some more soup? There should be some bread in the cupboard above the fridge."

I sit down and wait for Kat-copy to do the same. She sits at the edge of the sofa, tense and wary of the rest of us. Maybe we need to clear the room a little.

"Benjamin, can you check on your latest project?" I ask him, wiggling my eyebrows to convey the hidden message without alerting the child. "Maybe Ryker wants to come with you? And Lennox, wasn't there something you wanted to do?"

They follow my hint and leave us alone. Now it's just me and the girl. I can sense the others close by. I'd hoped that Benjamin would show Ryker his kittens, giving me peace of mind that the boy is coping with looking after them, but they stay in the room next door together with Lennox.

"I know this must be strange for you," I start, giving her a smile. "I remember how it was the first time my collar was taken off."

She frowns at me. "This isn't my first time."

Alarm bells start to ring in my head, but I push them away. "No?"

"They make me shift all the time. Grandma Doctor says that it's good for my body to shift as often as possible."

"Grandma Doctor?"

"You don't know her?" Now she's starting to look at me as if I'm stupid. "She said she raised you, just like me. She told me all about you."

Okay, now I'm officially confused. I wasn't raised by anyone. There wasn't one person responsible for us at the Pack, especially not someone we'd ever dare call grandma. We had trainers, teachers, masters, but none of them ever took a particular interest in me. There were some doctors and researchers who studied me, trying to figure out how I was different from the wolves, but I don't think any of them was a woman.

"What did she tell you about me?" I ask cautiously.

"That you're a rebel," she answers immediately.

"That you're planning to destroy us all because you're jealous of our family. You're angry that they expelled you, so now you want to seek revenge."

For her age, she's using some pretty big words. It sounds like she's regurgitating what this Grandma Doctor told her.

"She said you'd be very alone and sad," the girl continues. "And that by bringing you home, I can help you be happy again."

I smile again, trying to put as much happiness into it as possible. Even though it's hard to smile at all the stuff she's saying. It's disturbing.

"I'm happy already," I tell her. "I have my own family here. And I wasn't expelled, I left because I no longer wanted to stay with the Pack."

She's quiet for a moment. "The other cat, is he your family?"

"Ryker? Yes, I think he is."

"How can you not know?"

I sigh. "I only met him a short while ago, but he's become an important part of my life, so yes, he's family. As are all the other people you saw here."

Bethany enters with a large tray and I point at her. "That's Bethany. She's been living with me for a few months now. She's great at cooking. You'll see when you try her hot chocolate."

"You can call me Beth." She smiles as she hands Mini-Kat a mug. She's topped the cocoa with a massive hood of whipped cream, clearly trying to get some meat on the girl's bones.

Also, Beth?! It took four months before she told me I

could call her by her nickname. And now she's offering it to the clone. No, I'm not jealous. I don't really care. But it's not fair.

Kat sticks out her tongue and carefully licks the cream. Her eyes widen slightly when she tastes it.

"Good?" I ask, wishing Bethany had given me some hot chocolate too rather than the mug of tea she's now handing me.

The girl doesn't respond, instead she greedily starts slurping the cocoa. If copious amounts of hot chocolate can get her on our side, then so be it. I'm not beyond bribery, on the contrary. It's a great method to get what I want.

Gryphon joins us and puts several bowls full of soup on the living room table. He probably assumed that everyone else was still here.

"Do you want me to leave?" he whispers while Kat is occupied with her drink.

I nod and he quietly moves away, leaving me stuck with his scent in my nose. I really need to figure out what he is; it's driving me crazy. There's something not-human in his scent, but not strong enough to identify. It's the same as with Lily, although I always thought it was her multiple layers of perfume that changed her scent. Now that I know about her succubus nature, it makes a lot more sense. Succubi are closer to humans than shifters, so her scent is very similar, with just a touch of extra spice. If she hadn't told me that there are no incubi, I would have almost thought that Gryphon is one of them. He's certainly got the looks, even with the scars across his face. It would also explain the feeling I get in the pit of my stomach every time he's close to me.

"Could I have more, please?" Kat asks sweetly, smiling at Bethany. The two of them seem to be quickly turning into friends. Unless this is all an act and my clone is scheming to deceive us for now, only to turn on us at the perfect moment. I don't know what to think of her. She's a child, she looks innocent and cute, but she's been raised by the Pack, which means there can't be much innocence left in her. The smile she gives Beth seems genuine though.

"I'll make you another mug," my friend promises and leaves for the kitchen. I'm alone again with my mirror image. Mini-Kat. Clone-Kat. Fake-Kat. I wish they'd at least have given her a different name. This is too creepy.

I swallow my discomfort and smile. "Would you like some soup?"

The girl shakes her head. "I don't want to spoil the sweet taste with saltiness."

I chuckle. "Very wise. You can have some soup later, if you change your mind. I tried some earlier, it's delicious."

Remembering how yummy it was, I take a bowl and eat a spoonful, both because I'm hungry and because I want to seem relaxed. I still don't believe that this is nothing but carrot, parsnip and parsley. There must be some kind of hidden ingredient.

"They told me you were evil," Kat says out of nowhere. "But you don't look evil."

I almost choke on my soup. "That's because we look the same. Are you evil?"

She frowns, scrunching up her face as she thinks. "I don't think so."

"Good, then so neither am I."

"But why would they say that?" she asks, genuinely confused. Poor thing. The fact that she's questioning it gives me hope, but I think we'll have a long way to go.

"They don't like me very much at the Pack," I explain. "I didn't always follow the rules."

"I don't either," she whispers, giving me a tiny smile. "But it's hard not to do what they say."

I nod. "The collar, right?"

"The silver collar takes away *me*, but when I wear the yellow one, I can think."

Okay, she's breaking my heart. Switching her collars makes it even more terrible. She knows the difference, knows how they're erasing her free will when she wears the silver collar. She might be young, but she understands much more than she should at her age. I wonder if that's because she's a clone or because of the way she's been brought up.

"Does the silver collar prevent you from speaking?" I ask gently, and she nods.

"It's like a dream. I sometimes see things, but I can't act. The collar takes over and I'm stuck inside."

"Do they make you wear the silver collar a lot?"

Again, she nods. "They say it's because I'm all grown up now. The yellow one is only for children."

I don't tell her that she's still a child. I doubt she'd believe me. She actually sounds proud of the fact that she gets to wear the silver collar rather than the bronze one, unaware that she's the only one who has such a collar. Unless the Pack have completely changed in the past seven months, but I doubt that. I sometimes see Pack assassins from afar, their collars hidden under scarves or upturned collars, but sometimes the bronze, almost golden colour shines through. I would have noticed if they'd switched to silver ones.

"Kat, I need to ask you something important. Do you remember going into a large factory yesterday?"

I don't think she could scrunch her little face up any more than she is now. She's trying very hard to remember, that much is obvious. "The smell... it was like the mug."

"That's right. It's an old chocolate factory. It did still smell of cocoa, a tiny bit."

"I remember the smell, but I don't know what happened. I think I saw a cat. Maybe?"

I don't think she's lying. She must have been wearing the silver collar, which means that she wasn't in control. I let myself relax a little more. She didn't consciously murder the cats, although this also shows that she's capable of killing when she wears that collar. She'll be programmed to do any violence necessary, and she wouldn't be able to stop herself. Luckily, that collar is off now and I'll be damned if I ever let anyone put it back on her. Even though she's my clone and not my little sister, I'm starting to feel a little protective of her.

"Do you remember anything after that?" I ask her. "How you got to the shed we found you in? What happened to the cats?"

"Shed?"

Ah, of course, she won't even know where we first saw her.

I get up and go on my knees in front of her, now confident that I won't scare her, and that she won't attack me. "I think the collar made you take some kittens," I explain gently. "Don't worry, we don't blame you, it wasn't you who did it, it was the collar. But those kittens are missing and we need to find them. Can you remember anything that might help us? Anything after you smelled the chocolate?"

"I don't think so," she says, looking at the floor.

Bethany chooses the perfect moment to return. She carries another mug of hot chocolate. I get up and take it from her, ignoring her protest. I hold it in front of Kat, letting her breathe in the scent.

"Close your eyes. Remember the smell. Sweet, delicious chocolate. Can you remember it?"

To my surprise, she really closes her eyes and her expression relaxes. She's probably so used to following orders that she doesn't think twice about it.

"It was dark," she whispers, before drawing in another deep breath. I hold the mug as close to her nose as I can without burning her.

"Yes, it was dark," I encourage her. "Was there anyone else? Did you hear anything?"

She stays quiet for a moment, her deep breath the only sound. I appreciate that she's trying. I think she wants to please me, make us happy. I doubt she's ever been treated with kindness, or been thanked. Once this is over, I'm going to make sure she gets chocolate every single day. And never wear a collar again, obviously.

"Meow."

She doesn't say it as a human word, she makes the sound like a cat would. Suddenly, Ryker's in the room, running towards her with panic in his eyes. I know why, I recognised the voice. Pumpkin. She's echoing pumpkin's words. Being human, I don't understand exactly what he's saying, but it's easy to hear the anguish in the sound. He's begging to be released, to be let free. He'd probably seen Mila and Haru slaughtered by the time he made that sound. He's scared, desperate.

Ryker meows in return, but Kat doesn't respond. She keeps her eyes closed, seemingly lost in the memory. Ryker looks at us, probably not sure what's going on. I put a finger on my lips and he nods.

When Kat stays quiet, I move the mug back and forth, making steam swirl up in lazy spirals.

"You saw cats, am I right?" I ask quietly. I don't want to disturb her, but I also don't want her to get trapped in her own mind. I know how confusing it can be once you take off the collar. It's like a part of your personality is returned that you'd forgotten about.

"Little cats," she whispers. "She took them. They didn't want to leave me, but she needed them."

"She?" I ask, a little too sharply.

"Grandma Doctor." She opens her eyes wide, terror reflecting in their depths. "I remember."

CHAPTER FIFTEEN

We've left Kat with Ryker. She's exhausted and I hope she's going to be able to sleep a little. The rest of us are in my office, crammed into a room too small for this many people.

When I first moved in here, I found a whole stack of files waiting for me. Most of them were about important people in the town; a summary of their strengths and weaknesses along with any other information that might come in handy. I never found out whether Mystery Man created them himself or got them from someone else, but they sure came in handy several times. It saved me time and effort. Now, we've each got a pile of files in front of us, hunting for a woman who's working with the Pack. I've never looked at all the folders, but I know there are several documents about Pack members. I've mostly ignored them, not wanting to revisit the past. If you go against one member of the Pack, chances are that you'll have to fight them all, and until now, I've always wanted to avoid that.

Not anymore.

"Women are very much underrepresented in the criminal underworld," Bethany observes after leafing through half her stack.

"Not at Meow, we're an equal opportunities business," I quip. "Equal deaths for all."

But she's right. Most of the files I've looked at are about men. At least that makes it a lot quicker.

"Kat, do you remember the deer shifter?" Lennox suddenly asks.

I look up from my current folder. "Deer shifter?"

He nods. "It must have been shortly before you arrived at the Pack. She was a couple of years older than me. No idea where they found her, but they brought her to the headquarters and put a collar on her. First deer shifter they'd ever seen, I think, judging from how excited everyone was. She stayed in our dorm for one night while they were waiting for some special scientists to arrive. Didn't say a word, totally frightened. We never saw her again, but I remember when they came to collect her in the morning. There was a woman there, one I'd not seen before. She was tall, taller than most of the men with her, and she was wearing a white lab coat. I only remember her because she was the biggest woman I'd ever seen and I was wondering what kind of animal she was." He grimaces. "That was before I learned that not everyone has an animal inside of them."

"You actually thought that?" Bethany asks, quirking an eyebrow.

Lennox shrugs. "I grew up with wolves, and then

with the Pack. I never knew any different. I only really entered human society when the Pack sent me on my first jobs."

"The people looking after you at the Pack, were they shifters too?" Gryphon asks. I forgot he was never part of it.

"No," I reply. "Some of them, but very few. I think only a handful of the top Pack members are shifters, and those weren't like the rest of us. They weren't living with the Pack because they'd been taken from their families. They'd joined as adults, voluntarily, because they wanted power. They didn't need to wear collars, and they treated us like scum. Worse than some of the humans, for some reason."

"I think some of the leaders weren't completely human," Lennox adds. "But I never found out what they were."

A muscle twitches near the bottom of the largest of Gryphon's scars, but he immediately manages to hide his reaction. Interesting. Maybe he thinks they might have been the same species as him?

"Do you remember how old the woman was back then?" I ask Lennox. "That would give us a hint on how old she is now. Just because Kat calls her 'grandma' doesn't mean that she's in her sixties or seventies. It could just be a title, or a joke even."

"No, she was quite old," Lennox says, his eyes unfocused as he tries to remember. "I was young back then so everyone seemed older than they were, but I'd guess she was in her fifties or older? I remember she had some grey hairs framing her face, but not all of it was grey. The rest was... brown, I think. Light brown."

"By now she'd be all grey," Bethany says. She playfully twirls one of her own strands of hair in her fingers. "Or white. I think brunettes usually turn more white than grey."

"Alright, we're looking for a very large woman with white hair," I summarise. "Who may be a scientist or researcher. I don't think I ever saw someone like that when I was at the Pack, so I assume she isn't local. I'll ask Ryker if any of his cats have seen her out and about, but I doubt she'll be walking around town a lot, not if she's that recognisable and important."

Lennox sighs. "I don't think there's any way around storming the Pack headquarters. The girl remembered handing the kittens to that doctor woman, and the streets she's described sound like they're near the headquarters. There must be a building though that we don't know about, or maybe a hidden basement, something like that."

"When they did experiments on me, they always blindfolded me," I say, only remembering it when I say the words. "They didn't want me to see where they were taking me."

I shudder at the memory. I've tried to repress all that's happened at the Pack, but somehow, my walls are crumbling with every day that passes. I think it's got something to do with being surrounded by people who're trying to get past my barriers. Lennox in particular. He's dangerous and I've let him in far too deep. There's no repairing some of the damage he's wrought inside of me.

"We're not enough people," Bethany says, voicing my thoughts. "We can't just walk into the Pack headquarters, nor can we fight our way in and out. It's a suicide mission. Are we really going to do that for a bunch of kittens?"

I growl before I can stop myself. Beth lifts her hands in apology and my panther calms down.

"But you get what I mean, right?" she continues. "We don't have a chance in hell of making it out of there alive. If we had more information, we might be able to sneak in and somehow get the kittens, but we don't even know where they are, let alone why they were taken. We'd be going in blind and I don't think that's a good idea."

"Kat, a word." Gryphon's voice is serious, so serious in fact that I immediately follow him outside the room. He walks all the way down the hallway until we reach one of the spare guest rooms (not that we ever have guests). Just about far enough that Lennox won't be able to hear us. Clever.

He closes the door behind us and sits on the corner of a dust-covered bed. "I need to tell you something," he says quietly, not meeting my eyes.

I sigh. "Please tell me this is important."

"It is, trust me. Sit down, will you?"

Curious, I take a seat next to him. His heart beat is picking up and he's starting to sweat. What is he about to tell me? It has to be bad if he's getting this nervous. I've never seen Gryphon nervous, never.

"I know a few things about the Pack that might help us," he begins. "But you need to promise that you won't tell the others how you know. None of them. Nobody, ever."

He looks up and locks eyes with me. His gaze is intense, pleading with me. At the same time, there's a threat hidden in their green, promising revenge should I go back on my promise.

"Alright, I promise," I say, feeling like this is an important moment somehow.

"When we first met, you asked me what I was," he mutters, now looking back at the floor. He seems very uncomfortable.

"I did, and you've refused to tell me every single time I've asked."

"Yeah, well, there's a reason for that. In retrospective, it may not even have mattered, but I wanted you to trust me, needed you to trust me. Which is why I stayed quiet."

I sigh impatiently. "Out with it. What are you? Why would it make me distrust you?"

He echoes my sigh. "You promise?"

"I swear it on my life."

"I'm... I'm a siren."

Alright, I was not expecting that.

"A what?"

"A siren. Please tell me you've heard of us?"

I shake my head. "The only sirens I know of are mermaids, and you don't really look like that. No tail, no scales, no scallop shells on your boobs. Definitely not a mermaid."

My eyes linger on his chest, where his boobs would be if he had any. Instead, there's only hard muscle that presses against his tight shirt.

He laughs softly, but it's not a happy sound at all. "We're not mermaids. We often get confused with them, but we don't live in water, only close to it, sometimes."

"But what do you do?" I ask in confusion. "What can sirens do?"

"We control people, mostly. That's our skill and our curse. We can influence human minds, steer them in directions they wouldn't usually venture. We can make a person fall in love with us, or make them kill themselves. If we tell someone to give us all their money, they will do so with a smile. We're manipulators, Kat. We control whoever we want to control, even shifters."

I jump up and fight against my panther who's trying to claw her way out of my body. She senses the fear that's running through me.

He holds up his hands with a smile so full of sadness that my fear instantly reduces.

"Not you, not any of you. I've renounced my family's ways. They revel in the power they have over others, while it's always scared me. I see it as a great responsibility, they see it as their right."

"Shifters..." I mutter. "The collars? That's the sirens' doing?"

He nods, anguish drawn across his face. "We can't influence shifters as easily as humans, so we had to find a way to amplify our power. No, not we. They. I was a part of it, yes, but only until I was old enough to realise what they were doing. I left as soon as I had a chance."

"Which is why you're not a doctor," I mutter, randomly remembering that fact.

"Yes, exactly. I didn't just leave the university before graduating, but I also left my family. I came to this town instead, hoping to escape their rule, but as soon as I arrived here, I realised that there's another siren clan controlling the city."

"The Pack," I whisper.

He nods grimly. "Lennox was right when he said that the Pack's leader aren't human. They're sirens, like me, and they've done the same thing here that my family did in the city I grew up in. It seems to be the curse of the sirens. Taking control, becoming the slavers of humans and shifters. We stay in the shadows, we pull the strings, but even though nobody knows it, it's us who're in charge."

My head hurts. He's deceived us. Lied to us. Lied to me. I was just about to trust him and now, I have no idea what to think.

"You're about to push me away," he says sadly. "And that's your right. But first, let me help."

I glare at him. "Kat's collar. You could have opened it. Instead, you let her suffer. She almost killed Benjamin because of it! How could you!"

I have a knife in my hands before he can even react. Anger flows through me, white burning rage that makes me want to stab him over and over again.

"No, you misunderstand," he protests. "I don't know how exactly the collars work. We didn't have collars where I'm from, they used implants that were inserted close to the shifters' hearts. I know what the collars do, how they bundle our powers, but not how exactly they function. With a bit of time, I could probably figure it out, but I could have hurt the little girl by doing so. Waiting for Lennox and the key was the safer option."

I don't want to hear his reasoning.

I thought I could trust him. I almost let him in. Almost thought he could be my friend. In dreams, even more than a friend.

I got it wrong.

So I stab him.

CHAPTER SIXTEEN

Alright, so I try to stab him, but he's faster. If I'd really wanted to hurt him, I would have, but I let him deflect my attack. The blade grazes the skin on his forearm, drawing blood. It's just a scratch though.

"I deserve that," he mutters.

I nod. "You do. And more."

He hangs his head, visibly ashamed of himself. That's a good start at least. Stabbing him has made my anger evaporate.

"How can you help us?" I ask and he looks up at me in surprise.

"Didn't you just tell me to leave?"

I shrug. "For now, you may be of use to us. If the people in charge are also sirens, we have an advantage if we have you on our side. Do they know you're in town?"

He nods. "Yes, but I doubt they see me as a threat. None of them have approached me; maybe they think I'm on holiday here. They know that if I was here in an official capacity as a representative of my family, I would have contacted them."

"I need to know more about sirens. How do I recognise them? What are your weaknesses? Can they exert control over me without a collar? And what about Benjamin and Bethany? They're human, will it be safe for them to be there with us or could they be turned against us?"

"We look human, although the chances are that we're prettier than most of them. Unless you're mauled by a bear." He points at the three long scars on his face. "We don't heal as fast as shifters, so we scar quite easily. Physically, we're weak, and many of my kind don't see a reason why they should learn how to defend themselves when they can simply tell their enemies to leave them alone. I'm an exception, but I've always hated having those powers. So there won't be many who can deflect a blade in the way I just did."

"It was a pretty good move," I admit.

"It's unlikely that many of the sirens in the Pack can defend themselves properly. But as you rightly said, the two humans will be easily susceptible. I don't think it's a good idea to take them with us. There are ways to train your mind to withstand a siren's call, but we don't have time for that."

"So it's just Lennox, Ryker, you and me."

"The cat is coming too?"

I shrug. "He's always been of help, and he has a network of cats all across the city who might be able to give us information. Not that I can actually talk to him right now, but still, better to have him along. The kittens might be scared and confused when we find them."

"Okay, so it's the four of us. Not the best odds considering we're trying to not only break into their headquarters, but also leave with a bunch of kittens."

"It's what we have to do."

"Yeah, I get that. And trust me, I don't want anyone to suffer at the hands of my people. They - we've done enough damage already."

The sadness in his expression makes me lose all my remaining anger. He seems to be a victim of his upbringing. That he chose to leave is a sign that not all hope may be lost. Yes, he deceived me, but I do that a lot too. I frown. When did I become so tolerant? So nice? The old Kat would have probably killed him by now. Instead, I'm considering letting him stay once we've completed our mission.

"You asked whether they could affect you without a collar," he says hesitantly. "Normally, we have barely any power over shifters, but because you've worn a collar for most of your life, you may be more susceptible. The only way to find out is if you let me try it on you."

"You want to enchant me?"

He laughs humourlessly. "I guess you could call it that. It won't hurt, you won't even know that it's not your own free will."

"That's scary."

He nods. "But would knowing that you're being forced to do something be better? At least this way, you're happy and without the knowledge that there are enemies all around you."

I scoff. "Yes, it would be better. It would give me a reason to fight, not simply follow orders without realising how I'm actually a slave. At least with the collars, it was obvious. Hard not to notice that you're someone else's possession if you're wearing a collar around your neck."

His expression turns even more pained. "I'm sorry for what my people did to you. It's wrong and I'm going to do my best to make it right. I didn't have any allies in my own city, so I was never able to change things. Here, I'm not alone. We can do this, we can break their hold on shifters and set them free. Maybe not immediately, but we can work against them, weaken them, until we're ready to take off everyone's collar and make them rebel against their masters."

"Did you know there are some shifters who like wearing a collar?" I ask him and he looks genuinely surprised.

"Why would they like it?"

"It gives them a sense of purpose. Being part of something. Some see the Pack as their family. They may not be there voluntarily, but they get used to it and even grow to like their lives. Stockholm syndrome, I suppose."

A kitten meows in the room upstairs and I remind myself that we better hurry up. We don't know why the Pack want the kittens, and they could be in danger. Or dead already.

"Try it," I say, meeting his eyes. "Do your siren thing."

"Alright. I'm going to make you do something that

you wouldn't otherwise do, that way we know how well my powers work on you."

"Just don't make me kill someone important," I warn him, and he laughs.

"You like killing. That wouldn't prove anything. No, I think I've got an idea..."

"It works better if we're touching," Gryphon says. "Hold my hand."

I shake my head. "No, I doubt the Pack sirens are going to get a chance to touch me. I need to know if they can do it without physical touch."

Although... he holds out a hand and I look at it. Maybe I should do it after all. Just to see what it feels like. I reach out and entwine my fingers with his.

His skin is warm, his palms calloused from fighting. Just like my own. We're so similar. Made for each other. Lennox is my opposite, a canine. It was a mistake to even think I could be with him. Dogs and cats can't be together. But Gryphon... he's an assassin, he's clever, he's got a great sense of humour, he looks amazing. He's perfect.

I step closer and put a hand on his chest. The muscles there are just as hard as I imagined. He must be ripped underneath that shirt. I want to see it, so I let go of his hand and start unbuttoning his shirt. He doesn't say anything, but a smile begins to form on his lips. He wants this too, it's clear from the heat in his eyes, the way his mouth parts slightly, the drum beat of his heart. Undoing the buttons takes too long. I rip open his shirt, exposing his bare chest. He's gorgeous.

I run my hands over his pecs, admiring the taunt

strength beneath his skin. He's a killer. Like me. I step even closer until my body almost touches his. He's so warm, so tempting. I want to lean against him and let go of my fears and concerns. Just a woman with a man. Unravelling in each other's arms.

But my conscience is too strong. We can't do this, not now anyway. We've got a job to do.

"Not now," I whisper hoarsely and using every ounce of willpower I can muster, I step back.

I meet his eyes, and even though we're no longer touching, the heat in his is increasing, drawing me in. I could look into those green eyes all day. They're a little too bright to be called emerald. A grassy meadow on a sunny day.

"That was strange," he mutters.

And just like that, the spell is broken.

"Strange? You call it strange when a woman rips off your shirt? Do you need an instruction manual to figure out what that means?"

I cross my arms in front of my chest and glare at him. I thought he was feeling the same, no, I *know* he did, so why is he being weird?

He sighs deeply. "You didn't fight my siren power. You changed it, and then you simply removed it not by struggling, but by finding a logical reason for why you couldn't accept it just now. That's never happened before."

"Wait, you..."

This time, he lets me stab him. Granted, I only nick his skin because I don't really want to hurt him, but I hope he gets the message. Don't mess with Kat, especially not with emotional stuff.

He groans, but doesn't even move to press a hand against the cut on his upper arm. Blood seeps into his dark shirt, but not enough to be worrying. I forgot he doesn't heal as fast as me. Oh well, it's a just punishment. Hopefully, it will scar. That will teach him not to mess with my head.

"You misunderstand," he says, eyeing his wound. "I didn't make you rip off my shirt."

I glare at him. "I certainly wouldn't have done that out of my own volition."

"Yes, you would have."

"Don't make me stab you again," I snap. "I'm not that kind of woman. I don't undress random men."

"Random?" He quirks an eyebrow. "I thought we were getting to know each other."

"Yes, while you were lying to me." I scoff. "I shouldn't have let you do that. Maybe I should cut off your dick, that will teach you."

He cringes. "I know you might not believe me, but not all men think with their cocks. I only used my power to make you hold my hand. I know you're not big on touching, so I thought that would be a good start. Then I was planning to have you take off your shirt-" I growl but he ignores me, "-but instead, you changed the command and took off mine. Do you see? While you didn't realise it was me telling you what to do, you instinctively changed the order to something similar but less damaging. It must be your experience with wearing a collar. I assume you were good at looking for loopholes in your instructions?"

I nod. "Very."

"That explains it. I was about to stop my powers when you managed to free yourself by deciding that this wasn't the time. Again, you instinctively knew how to get around it. If you'd simply tried to fight my command because you didn't want to do it, it wouldn't have worked, or at least it would have been very difficult. But by making it about the others, about our mission, you managed to break my influence without even knowing what you were doing. It's remarkable, really."

"Are you saying that I wanted to see you naked?" I stutter, my mind swirling. He must be lying.

His frown turns into a grin. "Yup. And I can totally see why."

He makes his pecs dance up and down. Okay then. Now he's getting a little cocky, but stabbing him a third time might be over the top. I need him in good condition for our mission. The cats depend on me. The heat that has gathered in my lower body dissipates as I think of poor little Pumpkin. It's been a whole day now since he was taken. Anything could have happened during that time. He might be dead and dissected by now.

Gryphon sees my expression and turns serious. "At least we know now that you can defend yourself against siren powers, even though it's in rather unorthodox ways. I'm not sure about Lennox though."

"He's been without a collar for ten years, surely that would make him less susceptible?"

Gryphon nods, although he doesn't seem entirely convinced. "Probably. He's strong, but I don't think he's as strong as you."

I'll take that compliment because I know it's true. Lennox may have some pretty good skills, but by staying at the Pack for ten years longer than him, I got a lot more training than him.

"Remember, you promised me not to tell anyone," he reminds me as I turn towards the door. "You can say that I've given you some helpful information, but no details. I don't want them to know just yet. You, I trust to do the right thing."

"What if I thought the right thing would be to tell them?" I ask, even though I'm not intending to break my word. I honour my promises, always.

"Then I would beg you not to," he says quietly. "I've had to fight what I am all my life, and finally, I am in a place where I can turn into the man I want to be. Please don't take that away from me."

My heart goes out to him. It was the same for me when I first left the Pack. I'd been defined by them, they'd given me a role that had become my sole purpose, so when I was suddenly on my own, I had to remake myself. I had to learn about who I was and what I liked. I'd never had the option to choose between different foods before. I wasn't sure if I preferred to sleep in single or double beds - which is how I ended up having a hammock. I didn't even know what size I wore because I'd always been provided my clothes. I'd felt so lost at the beginning, even though I'd never admit that. Right now, I see something of that Kat in Gryphon's eyes.

"I'm not going to tell them," I reply, fighting against the urge to reach out to him.

No, I've done enough touching for now. If that had really been me.

Yeah, who am I kidding. It had been me. And I'm regretting that Gryphon is about to put on a new shirt and hide the gorgeous view he's currently giving me.

Sacrifices have to be made. Sadly.

CHAPTER SEVENTEEN

I'm surprised when the others accept that I can't divulge what Gryphon and I talked about. What Benjamin and Beth don't accept, however, is that I want to leave them behind.

"No way," Ben says vehemently, glaring at both Gryphon and me. "I can't stay here while kittens are in danger."

"There are kittens in this house right now, Benjamin," I remind him. "If something happens to us, who's going to look after them? You need to stay here and make sure nobody takes the opportunity to attack our home while we're gone. That could be exactly what the Pack are planning. Lure us out, then burn down our headquarters while we're not there to fight them off."

He looks like he's about to protest, but Bethany puts a hand on his arm. "She's right. And there's the girl to think about too. Someone needs to look after her, and I'd rather that be the two of us than some of Ryker's cats. They wouldn't be able to deal with her should something happen."

I was debating whether to take clone-Kat with us, since she might be able to show us where to go, but she's in no fit state to come. If someone put a collar on her, she'd turn into our enemy, and now that we've got to see the girl underneath the collar, I wouldn't be able to hurt her. She'd be the perfect weapon against us. Maybe that's been the Pack's intention all along. Make us like the girl, then have her attack us.

"We looked through the remaining folders while you were gone," Lennox says, pointedly looking away from Gryphon's exposed chest. He's not meeting my eyes either, but it's clear to see that he's unhappy with me. I can almost feel his wolf cry out to me. I'm amazed that he's been this calm around me at all. I'd always thought that wolves would go into a frenzy until their mate agreed to be with them, but for now, he seems to have himself under control. I hope it stays that way, because I'm not going to turn into his one true love anytime soon. I need more time to think about him, and me, and us, but right now, there are far more important things occupying my mind.

"We didn't find anyone matching the description of this Grandma Doctor, but we did find a scientist with close connections to the Pack. In here it says that he's no longer in town, but Bethany is sure that she's seen him before."

My friend nods. "You know the herb shop on Smithy Road? I swear I bumped into him there. Literally bumped, because he wasn't looking where he was going.

It was maybe a week ago, so I bet he's still here. Maybe he never left and simply went underground."

Lennox hands me the file and I flick through it. There's not a lot information, but there is an address and a photo. He's in his late forties with a receding hairline and deep-set eyes.

"Doctor Alfie Lomond," I read. "Specialises in genetic engineering and selective breeding."

Bethany snorts. "As long as he's not doing any of the breeding. He's not my type, or any woman's type. Just look at those eyes, they're creepy."

She's right about that. With his hollow cheeks and sharp nose, he doesn't look like a man who I'd invite over for tea. Not that I ever invite anyone over, but that's not the point.

I check the date at the top of the file. It was compiled five years ago, which means he disappeared around the time my clone must have been created. Just a coincidence? I don't think so.

"Alright, let's go to his address," I say, ripping out the page with his photo and details and stuffing it in my chest pocket. "It's unlikely he still lives there, but it might give us some clues to his whereabouts. Definitely better than traipsing around the Pack headquarters looking for a hidden building. They'd take us out before we ever got close to finding what we're searching for. We may be better at fighting, but they outnumber us something like fifty to one, or even more. You know I'm confident in my skills, but not that confident. What we need is stealth and information, that's the only way this can work." I turn to Bethany. "Lock down the house. You know our emergency protocols. Let's be prepared for the worst. Benjamin, it might be safer if you get some of the other cats to help you with looking after the kittens. Talk to Ryker, he'll send some of his friends. I'll ask them to patrol the area as well and warn you if anyone from the Pack comes too close."

"Do you really think they're going to attack us?" Bethany asks.

"They created a young girl and turned her into a weapon. Right now, I want us to be prepared for anything. I've not worked hard for the past seven months to build us this home just for them to take it from me."

She gives me a sharp nod and I know that she'll follow the protocols we set at the very beginning. She's not going to underestimate the threat that's facing Meow. Even though I founded our company, they're more than just employees. They're part of it, they make it a home, a family.

I'm almost glad that Lily is away on holiday. One person less to worry about.

Wait a second. I'm worrying about other people. I'm actually scared that something might happen to them. When the fuck did that happen? When did I let them in, when did I let them become more than convenient accessories?

"Let's go and talk to Ryker," I say before my mind can shock me even more. Or maybe it's my heart. I'm discovering that I actually have one. It's scary.

THE HOUSE ALFIE LOMOND USED TO LIVE IN IS NOW occupied by a family. Their kids are noisily playing in a tiny garden, an even tinier dog running around their feet. Is that a toy or a dog? I shudder in disgust. Even a kitten has more self-respect than that jumping furball.

"I doubt we'll find anything interesting here," Gryphon says with a sigh. "Unless Ryker can smell something?"

The cat in question gives him a look that's full of a testosterone-laden challenge, and runs off towards the garden. Ever since Ryker saw Gryphon's torn shirt, he's been glaring at the siren. Is there something going on between the two of them? Being surrounded by so many men is getting exhausting. Give me a bunch of bitchy girls over these I've-got-the-bigger-one guys any day.

We wait in silence. A couple of Ryker's cats are following us covertly, but I could point to each one of them with my eyes closed. My panther senses are getting stronger again, but I don't think I'm ready to shift yet. If it's an absolute emergency, I might have to, but for now, I prefer to stay human.

"What if he doesn't find anything?" Lennox asks quietly when the cat still hasn't returned. "Do we just walk to their front gates?"

Luckily, we never have to figure that out. Ryker meows from afar and we move towards him in a trot. He's two houses down from where the children are playing in the garden. Thank goodness, away from that tiny barkmachine. I was close to eating that dog just to shut it up.

Ryker is waiting for us in front of a shed. Not

another one. What is it with us and sheds? I don't think I've ever been in one before, and now this is the second in as many days. Plus, Mr Kindler had one too. Maybe I should get my own shed, just in case. Interesting things seem to happen inside of them.

Ryker knocks his paw against the wooden door.

Gryphon steps forward and removes the rusty padlock with one sharp pull. Before he even opens the door, the stench of human waste fills my nose and I gag. Has someone been using the shed as an outdoor toilet? Not what I was expecting at all.

It's dark inside, but I let my eyes adjust and take in the scene. There's a man sitting on the mouldy wooden ground in the centre of the shed. He's naked, but he's so covered in dirt that it doesn't really matter. He's also missing one ear. Lovely. A torture victim, unless he's a Van Gogh impersonator.

He keeps his eyes closed but cocks his head at the sound of us entering his shed. The floor is caked in human waste, confirming that it's been indeed used as a toilet, except that I hadn't anticipated that a man is living *inside* the toilet. What a strange situation. He's thin, but not starved; someone is keeping him alive. They're not taking good care of him though, judging from the matted hair and his long, curved fingernails.

"Who are you?" I ask and the man turns his head towards me.

He doesn't reply. Of course not. That would be far too easy.

I sigh and pull one of my knives. "Tell me quickly,

I'm not very patient right now. There are children in danger so you better talk before I get angry."

He doesn't open his eyes, but he does open his mouth. A gaping hole sits where his tongue once was. He won't be able to tell us anything.

"Can you understand me though?" I ask and to my relief, he nods. Somehow, we're in the same situation as with the clone girl. While we managed to get her talking, I doubt there's anything we can do for this man. Cutting out a tongue is a pretty permanent solution to preventing someone from spilling secrets.

"Do you know the Pack?" I ask him. His eyes snap open, exposing bloodshot pupils that stare at me in shock. He slowly lifts a hand and makes a cutting motion in front of his throat.

"You're scared they might kill you? Honestly, wouldn't that be better than how you currently live?"

Ryker meows, but I don't think it's to agree with me. Oh shut up, kitty cat. I'm tired and impatient. I don't have time for this man to be scared.

"You know the Pack then. We're looking for a man called Alfie Lomond. Do you know him?"

I didn't think his eyes could go any wider, but they do. He looks to either side, as if he expects the Pack to attack him, then focuses his gaze on me, examining me from top to bottom. Usually, I'd relieve men who do that from the burden of their balls, but he doesn't do it because I'm a woman. I think he just wants to get the measure of me, find out whether I'd be strong enough to not get killed.

Finally, he nods, very slowly.

I'm hiding my relief at the fact that we might have a lead to follow. "Is he still alive?"

Again, the man nods.

"Is he the one keeping you here?"

A third nod.

"Do you know where he is now?"

This time, he shakes his head. Fuck. It was going so well.

"Alright, do you know where he works? We know that there must be some kind of hidden lab or research facility that the Pack run. Does that ring any bells?"

His eyes almost pop out of his sockets. His nod is almost imperceptible, but he does seem to know what I'm talking about.

"Someone's taken some friends of mine," I explain. "And there are things going on in that lab that we need to stop. If you show us the way, I'll make sure to keep you safe."

He laughs, a horrible gurgling sound.

"I don't think he wants to be safe," Lennox mutters from behind me. He steps forward to look at the man. "Do you want us to end your suffering?"

The prisoner stares at Gryphon for a long time. I can almost hear a conversation happening between them, but I'm sure I'm just imagining that. After what seems like forever, the man nods and carefully shuffles on his knees until we see his back. Thick red welts cover his skin, old marks from what must have been brutal whippings. They did that to us back at the Pack, but we healed. This man didn't.

His wrists are tied together. No wonder he's been

soiling himself. And even if he'd wanted to, he wouldn't have been able to take his own life to escape the pain, not tied up like this.

Gryphon produces a knife out of nowhere and gently cuts through the rope. Even when his bonds fall to the ground, the man doesn't move his arms. The way his shoulder blades curve strangely, he must have some dislocated joints. Poor man. Gryphon was right when he talked about ending the man's suffering.

I step back and let him and Lennox help the guy up. He's barely able to walk, but he tries to, one stumbling step after another. When the first ray of sunshine falls onto his face, he grins a toothless, tongueless smile and closes his eyes. I wish we could leave him here to enjoy the sun one last time.

Sadly, we need him to show us the lab or we'll never find Pumpkin and the other kittens.

"Is it far?" I ask him, almost regretting to disturb his moment of peace.

He nods, and I can't help but sigh.

"One of the guys will carry you. Try to take us the quickest route possible, although we can't risk being spotted, so avoid any busy streets. Got that?"

I have a feeling like we're making a mistake here, but there's no other way.

I prick the man with a sleep dart before Gryphon cuts his throat. Strategically, it would have made more sense to keep the man alive until we're sure this is the right place and that he hasn't led us into a trap, but his constant groaning is getting annoying.

He's guided us to an office block a couple of streets away from the Pack headquarters. We're hiding in an alleyway while Ryker and his cats check out the area. Two security guards are guarding the entrance of the building that the man gestured to be the one we need to enter. One of them is human, but the other is an uncollared shifter. Curious. Usually, only a very select group of Pack shifters are seen as trustworthy enough to be without a collar, and all of them are too important to be guarding a building.

The sun is setting and the shadows around us are growing. My favourite time of day. People are leaving their workplace, tired and eager to get home. They don't look at suspicious things they may have noticed in the morning when they were more alert. Now, they couldn't care less about what's happening around them. Soon, the streets will be empty, with only a few stragglers who worked late. In other parts of town, this is the time when the pubs get busy and the first drunks start to stagger around, but not here. This area is nothing but one office building next to another. Utterly boring and depressing.

While Lennox and Gryphon deal with the man's corpse, I am crouched on the ground, my eyes closed, focusing on the scents and noises all around us. The people around us are all human, that security guard the only anomaly. Most of the humans smell exhausted. I wonder if I do, too. There is still a weight in my limbs that is keeping me from being at full strength.

It shouldn't be hard to get into the building. All of us are good at climbing, and I'm sure we'll either find an open window or use the diamond saw I have stashed in my backpack. My instincts are telling me that we need to be careful though. I doubt these two men outside are their only security measures. I'm having trouble sensing the inside of the building, even though I should be able to from this distance. They must be using kholstone, a synthetic material that blocks shifter powers to a certain extent. Back at the Pack headquarters, they had some of the rooms clad in the stuff so that we couldn't hear what was going on inside, as well as the entire top floor where the leaders live. If they're using it here, that must mean that we're in the right place. They wouldn't bother using such an expensive material unless they had something to hide.

Less and less people are leaving the building, most

have long disappeared down the street by now. They'll be sitting at their dinner tables soon, maybe watching tv, talking about work, about how exhausted they are, how much they're looking forward to the weekend. I don't think I've ever had an actual weekend. I don't take off more than a day at a time. There are always people that need killing, and it's easiest to find them off guard when they're at home, relaxing.

I sense Ryker return and open my eyes, watching him sneak towards us. Nobody is taking a second look at the cat. He may be gorgeous and big for his kind, but he's still just a cat in their eyes. Ignorant humans. Cats are so much more advanced than them in some aspects, but of course they'd never accept that. The arrogance of cats is only beaten by that of humans.

"Have you found a way in?" I ask Ryker as soon as he's arrived. He nods, then meows. There's worry in the sound, but I don't quite understand what he's trying to say.

"Are you worried they might be expecting us?"

I feel his assent even before he bows his head.

"Well, they don't know what's coming for them," I say grimly. "We're going to get the kittens and make sure that my clone is safe from them." I turn to Lennox. "How do you feel about a little arson?"

He grins. "Thought you'd never ask."

His boyish enthusiasm makes me smile. He's always loved blowing things up.

"First, we need to find the kittens and get them out. Then we have to figure out what exactly they've been doing here. Take any interesting documents you come across. Once we're all done, we burn down the building. That should hopefully act as a blow against the Pack, even though it's not their headquarters. That will be a project for another day."

I resist the urge to rub my hands like an evil villain who's scheming to take down the government. The Pack isn't quite in charge of the town, but they do pull enough strings to have more power than they should. Who knows how much they control.

"What if the kittens aren't here?" Gryphon asks. I want to throw something at him.

"Let's think positive," I retort. "One step at a time. Ryker, can you get your cats to start some kind of fight outside the building? That should distract the guards for at least a short while. Lennox, you sneak around and prepare everything to start a big fire."

"Can it be an explosion?" he asks with a cheeky glint in his eyes."

I chuckle. "Whatever you want. Drench the building in acid, for all I care, as long as it's destroyed once we leave. Gryphon, Ryker, you're with me. Together, we should be able to sense the kittens, and if not, Gryphon might be able to use his special skills to ask one of the employees where they're kept."

The siren shoots me a warning glance, but he shouldn't worry, I'm not about to break my promise. His secret is safe with me.

"What signal are we using for me to start the fire?" Lennox asks.

Damn, I should have brought the walkie-talkies. I got them a while ago when I saw them on sale at a DIY shop, but never used them. I don't usually take people with me when I go on a job.

I shrug. "I could roar really loudly? By then, it won't matter if people know that we're there."

Gryphon snorts and pulls a whistle from his coat pocket. "Or we could use this. A little more sophisticated."

"Are you calling me unsophisticated?" I quip, pretending to be offended.

Gryphon ignores me and turns to Lennox. "Want some of my explosives? I brought some, just in case. They always come in handy one way or another."

Boys and their toys. I let them exchange dynamite while mentally preparing myself for the assault of the building. I really hope we're in the right place, but the kholstone coated walls are a good indication that there's something going on in there. Plus, the broken man was unlikely to deceive us. All he wanted was to be released from his existence of pain and misery. Poor guy. I wonder who he was. An ex-Pack employee perhaps? I might never find out. Urgh. I hate unsolved mysteries.

Ryker meows impatiently, and I get up from my crouched position, stretching my limbs.

"Show us the way in," I tell him. "Let's get your son back."

RYKER HAS FOUND A RUSTY VENTILATION SHAFT AT THE other end of the building, away from the guards, which means we don't have to use his cats as a distraction.

Lennox rips off the shaft's cover, his muscles rippling beneath his shirt as he does so. I look away. No distractions. Since he's the largest of the four of us, he goes last, with me first, followed by Ryker who's helped up onto the ledge by Gryphon.

I move slowly across the groaning metal, trying to make as little noise as I can, but since this shaft looks older than I am, that's pretty much impossible. Hopefully, most people will have left the building by now. Compared to me, Ryker is quiet as a ghost. Sometimes, being small comes in handy. There's a turn up ahead, but before I even get there, the groaning gets louder and suddenly I'm falling.

I land on all fours, thanking my cat instincts. I look up and stare at the massive hole in the ceiling. Oops. Guess that ventilation shaft wasn't made for people to crawl through. I dust off my clothes and wait until the others have climbed down. There are no sounds that would indicate people having noticed our arrival. I sniff the air. There's no kholstone anywhere around here, so we must be in one of the boring office parts of the building. I close my eyes to be able to focus better, and extend my senses. There's a faint trace of kholstone beneath us, and more a few storeys up, but a much smaller amount, probably just one room.

"Lennox, you go upstairs, there's a room there that might be of interest. Maybe check that one out before you go and lay your explosives. Ryker, Gryphon, we're going to explore the basement. There's something down there that they don't want us to smell."

"That they don't want *you* to smell," Gryphon

corrects. "I have no idea what you're even talking about. This is a human nose through and through."

I raise an eyebrow at him and he shuts up. Let's not pretend that he's human, that wouldn't be good for our currently slightly strained relationship.

"I'll be waiting for your signal," Lennox says and jogs off without another word.

"Ryker, can you smell the kittens?" I ask in the vague hope that his genetic connection to Pumpkin might give him an advantage. He shakes his head.

"Alright then. Basement it is. Let's be on our guard, with that stupid kholstone, I can't even sense if there are any people down there." I smirk at Ryker. "I almost wish you were a normal cat, maybe they're not affected by this like us shifters are."

He glares at me, then runs towards the staircase at the end of the corridor. A green emergency exit sign is flickering above the double doors leading to it. Ryker waits there, probably unable to push the heavy fire doors open himself. It must be so embarrassing to be a tiny shifter surrounded by big shifters. Like me. And Lennox. And I'm kind of counting Gryphon too because he's big, albeit not a shifter. Ryker is totally outpowered.

I pretend not to notice that he had to wait for us, and open the doors wide enough for him to slip through by my side. The staircase is dirty and smells of dusty concrete. Still better than taking the lift. I hate elevators, they make me feel out of control.

At the bottom of the stairs, a set of metal doors await us. I can't sense anything beyond those doors and it drives me crazy. I'm not used to having to rely on my sight alone.

Gryphon draws a curved sword from the sheath on his back and I do the same, tightly grabbing two of my favourite knives. I'm going to enjoy using them to cut up whoever hurt the kittens.

"Ready?" I whisper and check on the two men.

Gryphon nods and Ryker gives me a small meow. He extends his claws and arches his back, ready to battle.

"Let's keep at least one alive," I mutter. "We need information about what they've done to my clone and what else they've been doing. Once we have that, they're all fair game."

"I'm looking forward to it," Gryphon growls. Surprised, I look at him. His expression is fierce, his eyes full of excitement. He loves a good fight as much as I do. Or is there more? Does he want revenge for a child and cats who he doesn't even know? If so, it's proof that he's so much more human than I thought.

I remind myself that even if it's not his family running the Pack, it's still his kind. He must feel responsible for this at least in part. Sometimes, the biggest threats to a tyranny don't come from the outside. They come from their own creations.

I put my hands on the door handles and take a deep breath, getting in the zone. I'm still weaker than I usually am, but the adrenaline is helping in hiding that. I should be fine against normal Pack members, and for once, I'm not alone. It's strange fighting alongside other people. Well, one person and one cat.

With one more deep breath, I pull open the doors - exposing a long, boring, and very empty corridor. Well, that was a bit of an anti-climax.

We're silent as we walk further into the basement. There are no doors leading off on either side, just shiny metal walls. I wonder where the kholstone is that is stopping me from properly using my senses. Behind the walls? Somehow mixed with the metal? I've only ever seen it used as a paste that's painted on walls, but this part of the Pack seem to have more advanced technology than what I'm used to. The clone's collar was one example, this might be another.

At the end of the corridor, we have the choice of turning left and right. Gryphon signals that he'll take the right passage, and I nod in confirmation. Ryker stays with me and together, we turn left and hurry along yet another bland corridor.

At the end of it are three doors. This time, we have to decide on one. Carefully, I press my ear against the centre door, but I can't hear a single thing. They don't just block my shifter senses, but my human ones too. Ryker sniffs the ground and suddenly, his ears twitch and he grows tense. He points a paw towards the door on the right. He must smell something, but I don't. Nothing.

"Pumpkin?" I mouth and he nods.

While I want to storm in right away, I take the time to pull several sleeping darts from my collar and deposit them between my fingers, ready to throw. It's quicker than fighting my way through several people while trying not to hurt them too badly. As much as I want to kill them all, the rational part of my brain keeps reminding me that we need information more than revenge.

With my darts in one hand and a knife in the other, I slowly pull open the door.

Three men in lab coats are standing around tables, another one is sitting at a desk. All of them are turned away from me. Perfect. Someone else is moving behind a set of shelves that act as a room divider, but I don't have time to find out who that is.

I flick the darts, each one embedding itself in one man's neck. One guy manages to turn to me before he collapses to the floor - it's Alfie Lomond - while the others never even get to see their assailant. I'm going to enjoy killing Alfie later on for what he did to that shed guy. Maybe I'll make him shit himself first so that he can experience what it feels like. I wonder if I'll ever find out what the man in the shed did to be treated like that. But this isn't the time to ponder over such things.

Ryker runs off while I take my other knife and prowl into the room, ready for whoever else may be waiting for me.

The person behind the shelves must have realised what's happening. They're crouched low, hiding from me. As if that were possible.

I sniff the air and the scent of fearful sweat enters my nostrils. It's a woman and she's scared. Not nearly as much as she should be. There's another scent though, further away. Another woman, this one is older. Not a trace of fear from her. Interesting.

I make sure none of the men are moving and that there's nobody who I've overlooked in this part of the lab, then slowly prowl towards the shelves. It's a clever way to divide the room without adding walls. Maybe I should do that at home, split the massive dining room into smaller, more cosy parts.

Signs of being an adult: thinking of redecorating during the most inappropriate moments.

I feel the woman move long before she even gets close to attacking me with a pen. A pen. Seriously? Don't they have scalpels in this lab? Even scissors would be better than this. Such an insult.

I deflect her pathetic attack, then grab her wrist, twist it and flip her around until she's secure in my grip. She squeals, but I stab her with a sleep dart before she can start doing something as disgusting as begging for mercy. I let her fall to the floor, not caring if she'll get some bruises. She's working in a Pack lab, she can't be a very nice person.

With her out of the way, there's only one person left in this lab, unless there are others concealed behind more kholstone.

She's standing at the very end of the room, next to a small closed door. Her white lab coat stretches around her large figure, ending just below her bum, exposing thighs that could double as tree trunks. Seems they don't make lab coats in her size.

"Turn around, slowly," I snap, knowing exactly who this is.

Gotcha, Grandma Doctor.

CHAPTER NINETEEN

"You've found us then." The woman's voice is laced with poison and doesn't carry even a hint of surprise. "When K8 didn't return, I assumed she'd failed in her mission. Pity, she was showing such promise."

K8. Kat. My clone. She calls her by a number and that makes me incredibly angry. She's treating a little girl not like a person, but as a lab experiment. I'm going to make her suffer for what she's done, but not until I've got my answers.

"Sit down," I command, motioning towards a chair with one of my knives. The woman cocks an eyebrow, obviously not used to being told what to do, but she eventually does as I say.

I walk around her, my knife close to her neck the entire time. If she knows me, she'll know that I won't hesitate to strike. Keeping the blade there as a threat, I grab a pair of handcuffs from my backpack. They're some of my favourite tools. So versatile. Chaining someone to a chair is quite a boring use of them, but there's no time to play with her. Torture can come later, if she decides to resist.

When I've got her hands secure, I wrap some rope around her legs for good measure. I don't want her walking off anytime soon. Now that she's safe to be left alone for a moment, I sheathe my knife and walk over to the small door. Ryker is standing in front of it, one of his paws pressed against the steel. His eyes are so full of pain that I rip open the door as fast as I can.

He runs inside, meowing loudly. I listen for a reply, listen, listen, and yes, a faint meow. Relief bubbles up deep in my stomach as the first is followed by two more weak meows. The kittens are here!

"Oi, come here!" the woman shouts. "I don't have time to sit here all day."

I roll my eyes and return to her. "You know you're tied to a chair? You're going to sit here for as long as I want you to."

She glares at me. I'm amazed how there's still not a trace of fear in her eyes. She's either an expert at hiding it or she's simply not scared at all.

I drag another chair over and sit down opposite her. I'm sure that if Ryker needs my help, he'll call for me. He might already be cuddling his son.

"Who are you?" I ask, leaning back in the chair. It's surprisingly comfortable, even though it looks flimsy.

"Haven't you figured that out yet?"

I sigh. "How about some straight answers? You don't want to sit here for too long, neither do I. Just answer my questions and we'll be done quicker."

She raises an eyebrow. "And then? Are you going to kill me?"

"Potentially."

The woman smiles. "I thought so. I've raised you well."

I gape at her, then snort. "You've raised me? I don't think so. I've never seen you in my life."

Her smiles increases, but not in a good way. There's poison dripping from her eyes, exposing her twistedness. I need to be wary of her. She might be at my mercy physically, but I don't think she's weak nonetheless.

"Oh, you have seen me, my sweetie, but you won't remember. You were far too young for that. "

The tension inside of me is increasing, but I lazily stretch my arms and yawn. "If I wanted a fairy tale, I wouldn't have come all this way. Tell me who you are and what you're doing here."

"Now, wouldn't that be nice of me. It would save you so much trouble. But no, I don't think so. You can't make me talk."

Instantly, I'm on my feet with my knife touching the bottom of her chin. The lower one; she's got a big double chin. While most of her is bulk rather than fat, her face is puffy and lined with tiny red veins, like that of an alcoholic.

"Rest assured, I always manage to make people talk," I whisper into her ear. "In the end, you will be telling me everything I want to know. It's your choice how much it's going to hurt."

"I don't think you're going to hurt me," she says, her

smile still painted on her face. "Not when you know who I am to you."

I sigh dramatically. "I've been asking you who you are. Just tell me."

"Put that knife away and I might."

I slowly move the blade away from her chin, but not before making a small cut. She flinches, but immediately finds her composure again, looking at me as if nothing happened.

I swirl the knife in my hand a couple of times, making it very obvious that I wouldn't mind cutting her again. And again.

When she still doesn't start talking, I sit back on my chair again and wait. I'm going to give her that one chance, simply to make it easier for both of us.

"You were supposed to grow up here," she says, her smile lessening a little. "You were born in this very building and it was always the plan to keep you here, train you, study you, turn you into who we wanted you to be. Instead, your mother decided to be a rebel."

"My mother? She brought me here, I'd hardly call that being a rebel."

The woman laughs. "That was her returning you when she noticed that she wasn't going to survive for much longer on her own. She'd been on the run with you for four years. That destroyed most of our plans for you, obviously, since we missed out on some of the most important years of your development. The experiment turned into a failure before it had properly begun."

My mind is swirling. Experiment? My mother a rebel? What the fuck is this woman talking about.

Nothing of it makes sense, and I'm becoming acutely aware that I'm wasting time. We're here for the kittens and to find out about my clone, not about me. Lennox will be waiting somewhere upstairs, ready to set the building aflame. If we don't give the signal, he might come down to investigate. I should have brought those walkie-talkies. Next time.

"My bosses thought it would be enough to watch you grow, see how you developed even though we'd missed your childhood years. They didn't give me the funding I needed, not until they realised that you were too rebellious. You weren't of any use for our needs any longer, so we needed a replacement."

"Kat," I mutter. "The clone."

The woman laughs. "Kat? You gave her your name?"

"She gave herself that name," I snap. "Since you obviously didn't bother to give her one."

"Interesting," she mutters, looking around as if she wants to take notes. "How did you manage to speak to her? The collar should prevent that, unless it malfunctioned?"

I glare at her. She's driving me crazy. If my rational mind wasn't screaming at me, I'd have slit her throat by now.

"It didn't malfunction. We took it off."

For the first time, there's genuine surprise on her face. "And she's still alive?"

My heart drops. "What does that mean?"

"Previous clones rarely survived for long without their collars-"

"Previous clones?" I interrupt her harshly. "How many others were there?"

"With you, seven."

"Seven?!"

Then the penny drops.

She watches me with a smile as I realise what she just said. She's enjoying this. That's why she's telling me. This isn't about me getting answers, it's about her torturing me.

"Seven," I whisper. It can't be. I have a mother. I remember her, even though they are only fragmented memories.

"Was my mother-?"

"Was she the original?" The woman grimaces. "Yes, she was. One of our best non-collared shifters. I thought she was loyal, but seeing you, her clone, must have messed up her head. She took you and ran off, taking one of my lab assistants with her. The fool. He might still be alive if he'd stayed. We had to make an example of him."

My father. *Not* my father. Now I know why people sometimes faint when they get bad news. I feel light-headed, dreamy, not quite in reality. It's too much to take in.

"Why?" I snarl, pushing against my weakness, but the woman never gets the chance to reply.

A loud meow makes me jump up. Ryker!

I leave the woman cackling to herself and run into the other room. I never really looked at it earlier, I was too focused on what Grandma Doctor had to say. Now, I regret it. The room isn't as small as I thought, in fact, it's so long that it might be bigger than the lab. Shelves line the walls here at the front, stacked with glasses, vials and boxes. There are things swimming in liquid that I prefer to ignore. I'm not queasy, but this is too close to home just now. My thoughts are all over place, and let's not talk about my emotions. I'm a mess.

I race through the room until the shelves turn into stacks of cages. Dozens of small cages, each of them smelling of cat piss. Not all of them are full, and the doors of the lower two rows are open. Ryker is surrounded by six kittens, all of them trying to cuddle him to death. Their squeaky meows tear at my heartstrings and let me forget about my own troubles for a moment.

Ryker isn't looking at the kittens though. His eyes are on a cage at the very top. Pumpkin. The little cat is pressed against the bars of his confinement, crying for his father.

Ryker snarls at me to hurry, to reach up and get the cage since he can't reach it.

"You don't want to do that!"

The woman's voice makes me turn, even though I know that she's still tied to the chair and can't see what I'm doing right now. What an evil bitch.

"I will do whatever I want!" I shout back. While the kittens seem to be unhurt, my clone has been mistreated in this place. I don't know what happened to the other clones, where they are, if they're still alive, but I doubt they had very happy lives either. I'm going to take her apart for that, limb by limb. But first, I need to give Pumpkin back to Ryker.

Out of the corner of my eye, I see something flying towards me, but before I can react, it slams into me from behind, hitting the back of my neck. I sway, trying to find something to hold onto, but then cold metal touches my throat and everything turns black.

BURNING. SOMETHING'S BURNING. SMOKE FILLS MY lungs and I cough, trying to get it out, trying to breathe fresh air. I open my eyes, blinking several times as the smoke makes me tear up. Something feels different. Bad.

My mind is sluggish. What happened? Something about cats. Lots of cats.

I groan and try to sit up. My body won't move. It's heavy, so heavy, like it's not my body at all. There's no pain, yet it reminds me of my last shift, the one where I almost killed myself through blood loss. This isn't the same, but...

Meow.

Soft fur rubs against my arm. I turn my head, every inch a battle. Ryker is staring at me, his eyes filled with fear and worry. Slowly, my memories return. Pumpkin. The kittens. The woman.

"Pumpkin?" I whisper.

His anguished meow tells me all I need to know. He's not managed to free his son. Why is there fire? Lennox was supposed to wait until he got the signal. The smoke hurts my lungs and eyes, but I can't even lift my hands to rub away my tears. What happened to me?

Ryker meows again, but I can't understand him. Not

even his intention. No mental images. Nothing. All I can hear is a cat meowing. Yes, he sounds scared, but that's no surprise.

"What's going on?" I ask hoarsely. "What knocked me out?"

He takes a step closer and nudges my chest. No, not my chest, my throat.

Icy fear floods me. With every ounce of strength I have, I manage to move one hand to my neck.

Tears spring to my eyes and this time, they have nothing to do with the smoke.

They put a collar on me.

CHAPTER TWENTY

Ryker places his head on my chest, seemingly trying to comfort me. But there's nothing he can do to make me feel better. It's not the fact that I'm going to die that makes me want to scream. It's that I'm going to die a slave.

I thought I'd found my freedom. Created a new life for me. Now all that is gone, washed away like a dream, leaving nothing behind but the harsh reality. I'm a clone, I was always meant to be a slave. Those few months without a collar were just an illusion. It was foolish to think that I could escape the Pack.

Now I'm about to die. I didn't imagine it like this. I was always hoping for a warrior's death, killed by another assassin's blades. Going down in battle, adrenaline pumping in my veins, the thrill of the fight the last thing to feel.

Meow.

Oh fuck. Pumpkin.

"I'm sorry," I rasp. "I can't get up."

Ryker nudges me, presses his head against my ribs, but I think he knows that it's of no use.

The other kittens have gone; Ryker must have got them to safety. Hopefully, Gryphon and Lennox are safe too, away from the burning building.

"You have to do it yourself, Ryker. I can't help you, I'm so sorry."

I may be signing Pumpkin's death warrant, but there's nothing I can do. The collar has got me in its cold grip, sapping my strength, influencing my body and mind. I'm surprised I have any free will left at all. Maybe it takes a while to properly take effect. Not that it does me any good. I'll have to watch Pumpkin die before being killed by the flames myself. Or the collar, if it's faster than the fire.

Ryker gets up and tries to climb the stack of cages once again, but there's nowhere for him to put his paws. They reach all the way to the ceiling, so he couldn't even jump to the very top either. The howl breaking from his chest breaks my heart. It's the despair of a parent unable to save their child.

"Shift!" I shout at him, my voice getting weaker with every word. "Think of how you need to be tall, how you need to be human to save your son! You can do it, Ryker!"

The collar is trying to subdue me, turn me unconscious, but I'm fighting it with everything I've got, even though the pain is getting worse and worse. It's going to kill me, I know that. I learned that when the

Pack captured me shortly after Mystery Man had set me free. You can't put a collar on an adult shifter, even if they've worn one in the past. I don't know how long I have, but I doubt it's very long. Even if my body will stay alive for a few hours, my mind won't. Darkness is flickering at the edges of my vision.

Ryker is shaking, stretching, trying to reach his son, but he's not shifting. The desperation in his movement is like ice running through my heart, making me freeze from the inside. I want to help him, but I'm useless. There's nothing I can do but watch.

More and more smoke is gathering around us and the crackling of flames is getting louder. Soon, we'll be trapped in a sea of flames. Maybe I should ask Ryker to bite through my jugular before he leaves. Burning alive must be one of the worst deaths imaginable. Unless the collar kills me first.

Ryker howls in frustration.

"Think of your human side!" My voice is regressing to a hoarse whisper. It could be the smoke or the collar; either or, I'm screwed. We all are. I just hope the others get out alive.

"Think of what makes you human. What are the emotions that set you apart from the cats? What has always made you feel different?"

He turns and looks at me. Really, really looks at me. I wouldn't be surprised if he can see every single secret I hide at the bottom of my soul.

Then his face begins to twitch. His whiskers shiver, then retreat into his cheeks. His bones lengthen, his fur disappears, making way for smooth, dark skin. He starts to scream when his tail retracts. I avert my eyes, wanting to give him some privacy for some obscure reason. This might be the last time I ever see him. I should watch, share this moment, treasure it in the minutes I have left. But no, I listen to his screams with my eyes closed, hoping that it'll be over soon.

"Chhhrmm."

I blink open my eyes and look at the man in front of me. He's so different from what I imagined Ryker would look like. In my mind, he had blond dreadlocks, suntanned skin and blue eyes. In reality, his skin is the colour of my panther's fur, his hair is a dark grey just like the patch of fur on his chest when he was a cat, and his eyes... they're still the same. Bright yellow. He'll never pass as a human with those, but I don't care. They're stunning. *He* is stunning. Gorgeous. Impressive.

Since he's naked, I get the full view of toned muscle and lithe strength. Alright, I'm going to commit that sight to memory. He was larger than an average cat before he shifted, and he's larger than an average human, too. His shoulders are broad, his arms strong. Let's not talk about his abs. They might make me faint even before the collar does.

He looks at me for a second, then turns and reaches up to the cage containing Pumpkin. He doesn't even have to stretch this time.

I smile as he cradles the tiny kitten in his arms, looking at it with pure love. I'm so glad they're going to get out alive.

"Chrrrmmmmrrr."

He seems to be trying to speak, but this is the first time he's human, he must be totally out of his depth. I hope it's just a temporary thing. Even with this strangled, hoarse sound, I can already tell that his voice has a beautiful depth.

A rumbling sounds in the distance and the floor starts to shake.

"Run," I whisper. "Hurry."

I want to say more, so much more, but suddenly, there's a rope around my vocal cords, pulling hard. I can no longer speak. I try to, but not a single word passes my lips. The collar is winning. It's too strong.

All I can do is give Ryker one last smile.

Time to say goodbye.

Pumpkin meows and drums his paws against his father's chest. I wonder if they can understand each other. And does Pumpkin even know that Ryker is a shifter? So many questions that I'll never get the answer to. Dying sucks.

My vision dims. It's starting. Death. I've never much wondered about the afterlife, but if there is one, I don't think I'll end up in the place where the good people are. And if I end up with bad people... I'll probably come across some that I killed. Will I be able to kill them again? You know, just because?

My hearing is next to go. I still smell the smoke that's engulfing us, but I no longer hear the crackling of the flames, the groaning of the building. It's very quiet suddenly. I don't think I've ever experienced such silence. It's relaxing. I never realised how loud even my own breathing was. Now that all sounds are gone, I no longer feel that there's any point to fighting. I can no longer hear Pumpkin's meow. I can no longer see Ryker.

I feel his arms around me just before I can no longer feel my body. Is he carrying me? I wouldn't know. The smoke hides his scent. I hope he's not taking me with them. I would slow them down and there's no point to it, really. I'm mostly dead already. They'd never get me back home, where the collar key is, on time.

What I really hope is that he's going to kill the woman. Or let her burn to death, that's probably better. She deserves the pain of her flesh peeling off her body. I'm no longer going to feel it. My body is numb, just a piece of flesh that once housed me.

Is this the time when images should flash before my eyes, showing me memories from my life? If so, it's not happening. Maybe my life wasn't nice enough for that. I don't really want to see any snapshots from the time I was living with the Pack. Oblivion can have them. The only good times I had were those spent with Lennox.

My wolf. When he left, he took a part of me with him. I should have been overjoyed when he returned. I should have accepted the feelings growing between us. Instead, I pushed him away. Scared of commitment. Scared of losing my independence, of losing the life I'd built.

But what life was I even protecting? In the end, I was still doing the same that I did when I still worked for the Pack. Killing, thieving, making money. The only difference was that I did it for myself. How long would it have stayed satisfying though? I was so short-sighted. I put work first, ignored my heart. I guess I never learned how to act differently.

Lennox. I hope he survives, and I hope his wolf will get over the loss of his mate. If I were given a second chance, I'd change things. I'd give it a go. Be with him, at least for a while. See if I'm able to be in a relationship. And if it doesn't work, I'd still have two other men who've somehow wriggled their way into my dying thoughts.

Gryphon, a siren with a conscience. I've been attracted to him ever since he first appeared in my bedroom. My hormones get in a knot every time I see him. I've been ignoring it, but right now, it's the time to reveal my cards. Lay it bare. Accept what I feel. If not now, when?

And then there's Ryker, who's only been a man for mere minutes, yet the connection I've got with him transcends his humanity. I found him interesting and charismatic even when I thought he was just a cat, but ever since I found out that he's a shifter, I've seen him with different eyes. Seen the potential in him. We're so similar. So well suited. And now that I've seen his human body, well, it kind of underlines the point. He's made for me. Or me for him, since I'm the clone.

I'd laugh if I still had control over my body. I think my sense of smell has gone now too. No more smoke.

Am I burning already? Would I know? Or maybe I'm dead already and this is just an echo of consciousness. Maybe my mind is trapped in the collar forever.

Yes, think cheery thoughts, that's it. Positivity in death. Maybe that will make it a better experience.

I think I'm going crazy. Maybe I should concentrate on something specific to distract myself from dying. Meow. My friends. Bethany, Benjamin, Lily. I see them stand in front of our house, waving at me. Like they're saying goodbye. No, that's not very positive.

I move on, drawing on memories, but none of them is strong enough to keep my focus. I'm drifting, trapped inside my thoughts. That's enough to get anyone crazy, and I'm already slightly unhinged.

Maybe I should come up with something new, something that hasn't happened yet. And wouldn't happen.

Gryphon. Standing there with his shirt ripped open. Instead of turning away like I did in real life, this time, I pull him closer. Take off my own shirt. Kiss him.

It's so real that I feel his lips on mine, his breath dancing on my skin. It's beautiful.

"You know, I've always been more of a dog person," he whispers, his fingers tangling my hair.

I chuckle and slip a hand between his legs.

"I guess I will have to change your mind."

If I had a body, I might blush at my own words. Instead, I watch myself on the floor with him, fucking him on the carpet. He holds my breasts as he moves in me, and squeezes them with each thrust. It's making my chest hurt. And his lips are on mine again, but no, his head is nowhere near mine, so who's kissing me?

Rip. Like a curtain being thrown to both sides, exposing the stage, life enters me, and with it, light.

I open my eyes. I'm surrounded by people. This must be hell, specifically designed for someone as antisocial as me.

One person, one man, is closest to me, his hands hovering above my chest. Just where I felt the pain. Did he try to revive me? It feels like he crushed a couple of my ribs in the process.

I blink a couple of times and slowly, things lose their blurriness. Faces come into focus. Benjamin and Bethany are standing furthest away. Are they holding hands? Must be a trick of the light.

Lily is to my right, with a very human Ryker next to her. When did Lily get back? She was supposed to be away for another couple of days. Ryker's gently rubbing Pumpkin's head, who's stretched out near my feet. He's half asleep, lazily opening his eyes to look at me. He smiles, then goes back to sleep.

On my left is Lennox, his eyes leaking. Oh wolf, get a grip.

And then there's Gryphon, whose lips still seem to be touching mine even though he's standing now, stretching his back. He's got bruises on his face, but they're already fading. I must have been out for a while, even though it didn't feel that way.

My head is full of questions. How did we get out? How am I alive? Are all the bad people dead? But for now, I'm content to just look at the people around me.

"You made it," Lily whispers.

I smile at them all, rather happy to be alive.

"You're probably wondering what happened to you," Gryphon says, and I roll my eyes at him. Duh.

"We can do the long version later, but just to give you some peace of mind, the kittens are fine, the Pack building is completely destroyed, a couple of their people died, including that dreadful woman."

I should feel happy about that, but instead, I'm annoyed. I had so many more questions for her. Now, I'll need to find other ways to find out what happened. Who I am. What they did to me. Where the other clones are, if they're still alive. I went in there to get answers, and instead, I'm left with so many more questions than before.

"I'm sorry I had to start the fire before the signal," Lennox mutters, his eyes still wet. "They had me surrounded and I thought I wasn't going to be able to fight my way out of there. Setting off the explosives was the only way to distract them enough to get the upper hand. Annoyingly, the fire had everyone swarming around, meaning it took me forever to make my way downstairs. It was worth it though, I found some interesting things in that office, things that will help us in weakening the Pack."

I try to ask about the kittens, what they were used for, but my throat is too dry to even speak a single word. I point at Pumpkin instead, hoping that someone will understand what I want to ask.

Lily notices my predicament and returns with a glass of water a moment later. She tries to hold it to my mouth, but that would be too much loss of pride. I snatch it out of her hand, spilling most of it on the duvet, and manage to take two sips before my hand loses its strength. Not quite how I wanted this to look.

Pathetic. That collar must have damaged my shifter healing somehow. I must have been unconscious for a while, judging from Lily being back and Gryphon's faded bruises, so I should really be back to full strength by now. I hope this is only temporary.

"Turns out the kittens weren't stolen to get your attention," Gryphon says and I smile at him, glad he's got the message. "I found lab records, hundreds of pages of detailed observations on other kittens. They wanted to make the clones stronger by adding more cat genes. For that, they needed young cats, where the DNA isn't damaged by time. Of course they only wanted the strongest kittens for that, so they had them do all sorts of tests, strength, intelligence, perseverance. Luckily, they hadn't processed our kittens yet, or we may not have found them alive." He sighs. "We need more time to look through all the data I found to see if they succeeded with combining cat with shifter DNA."

"For now, you rest," Lily says, interrupting Gryphon's explanation. "You almost died. Gryphon may be the medical expert, but I'm prescribing you bedrest."

"Meow," I protest, unwilling to just lie here without doing anything.

They stare at me.

"Meow, meow. Meow."

"Ehm, Kat," Lily says, her eyes wide. "You're meowing."

I clutch my hands to my throat, willing my voice to return to human.

"Meow."

Oh fuck.

~ The End ~

❀ ❀ ❀ ❀ ❀ ❀

Kat's story continues in Purrr: books2read.com/purrr

Because reviews are almost as good as catnip, please make Kat happy and leave a review, even if it's just a few words.

ABOUT THE AUTHOR

Skye MacKinnon is a USA Today & International Bestselling Author whose books are filled with strong heroines who don't have to choose.

She embraces her Scottishness with fantastical Scottish settings and a dash of mythology, no matter if she's writing about Celtic gods, cat shifters, or the streets of Edinburgh.

When she's not typing away at her favourite cafe, Skye loves dried mango, as much exotic tea as she can squeeze into her cupboards, and being covered in pet hair by her two bunnies, Emma and Darwin.

Support her on Patreon and get exclusive benefits:
patreon.com/skyemackinnon

Subscribe to her newsletter:
skyemackinnon.com/newsletter

facebook.com/skyemackinnonauthor

twitter.com/skye_mackinnon

instagram.com/skyemackinnonauthor

bookbub.com/authors/skye-mackinnon

goodreads.com/SkyeMacKinnon

amazon.com/author/skye_mackinnon